DALLAS

★

BY WILL F. JENKINS

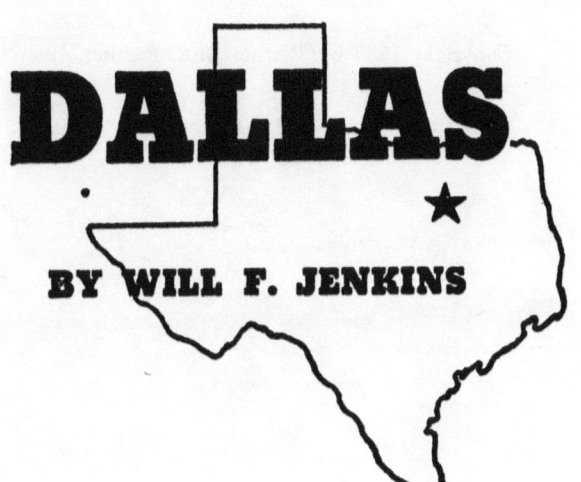

PUBLISHED BY BROWNSTONE BOOKS

Copyright not renewed.

Chapter One

FROM Texas on northward, it was clear that the world
had come to an end with Lee's surrender, but people
took the catastrophe in as many ways as there were people
to take it. There was, for instance, Colonel Blayde Hollister of the Fifth Georgia Cavalry. When he received the
notification that the war was ended, he called his regiment into formation and read the order. It seemed preposterous that the war could have ended without victory
for the Confederacy. It was plainly out of all reason that
the Fifth Georgia Cavalry should be ordered to surrender
itself to Yankee troops. But that they should actually do
so was unthinkable. So, standing very erect and pale
before the hot-eyed and hungry men who faced him,
Colonel Blayde Hollister formally disbanded his regiment, he being twenty-two years old at the time. And
then he started homeward with the empty feeling of a
man who has not been defeated, but who abruptly has
nothing left to fight for. He headed for his home, the
plantation near Valdosta, Georgia, where his father and
mother and sister would be needing him to face what
was bound to come, now that the world was at an end.
But he had some errands to do on the way.

All around him, as he traveled, there were the frag-
ments of the gamest army that ever fought battles on
empty stomachs. Some men headed straight home too,
grimly foot-slogging it or at the best riding battery horses
with only artillery harness for gear. Those men would
spade up neglected fields by hand, or plow the land doggedly in the same gray uniforms they'd worn in battle,
because they owned no other garments. Some would lin-
ger on the way, either because they were ashamed of
defeat or because they feared to find that they had lost
at home all that they'd fought for on many battlefields.
Some, of course, hardly changed their lives at all. They

3

would be guerrillas—Quantrell's men and the like. They
had robbed and looted before. They robbed and looted
now. And some former Confederates were headed for
lands overseas since the Confederacy was dead. The army
of the Khedive of Egypt for years to come would have
former Confederate officers in its higher ranks, and for
decades there would be no Central American revolution
in which the rebel yell would not rise from every jungle
fight.

But Colonel Blayde Hollister rode homeward, doing
his errands on the way. He did not think of going abroad
or keeping the field as a guerrilla. He rode steadily on his
good horse Yank—the horse being a prize of war—bra-
zenly wearing the full uniform of a colonel in the Confederate Army, which it was no longer legal to wear anywhere. He still made it a point in his own mind that he
had not surrendered; that he'd conceded only that it
would have been foolish for him and the other survivors
of the Fifth Georgia Cavalry to try to fight the whole
Yankee nation by themselves.

He stopped at one place to tell a young woman that
her husband had died bravely, and at another to tell a
gray-haired man that his son had been a credit to him.
Such errands delayed him, and he had many of them.
But as colonel of his regiment he could not well do less.

In the course of his message-giving he saw what had
come to pass at home in the Confederacy while its army
fought. It was not consoling. He could not guess what
his own family plantation would be like, with all the
Negroes freed and the state under a military government
that would presently change to a carpetbagger one, but
he knew that grim times lay ahead.

He could have taken off for Texas or the West, of
course. Plenty of men were doing that. But his father
and mother would need him, and there was his sister to
be thought of. When he'd gone off to war he was too
young to have a sweetheart. He had only a family. But
an extra man around home would be a stark necessity
in the troublous times ahead.

He was a long time on the way, but at the last he rode hard and fast. When he saw the first recognizable landmarks near the plantation he stopped—it was barely daybreak and he'd ridden all night long—and brushed off his uniform and made himself neat before appearing before his parents. He'd be coming home defeated but unashamed. He'd fought until the skies fell. And afterward he'd told the families of his fallen followers that their men had died bravely.

That was a comfort. He needed comfort now. On the last two miles toward home he rode through a woods path that was heartbreakingly familiar. He saw no one at all. Overhead the sun rose slowly and morning brightened with a vast deliberation. When he emerged from the last pine wood and his horse moved across dew-wet grass toward the clump of live oaks that surrounded his home, there was a lump in his throat merely from the sight of the place where he'd been born and the smell of the good earth of home in his nostrils.

There was the gate to the carriage drive. The fence was down and broken. He rode up the avenue of live oaks toward the house. Somebody had cut down half of them. But when he saw that, he saw much more. He did not look again at the desecrated trees. Instead, he rode slowly forward with his face first white and then a queer, stricken gray.

The house was ashes. It was no more than a heap of forlorn, scorched debris through which the chimneys reared gauntly upward. The very stables were burned—and Sherman's men had not been by this way, so it was not that disreputable substitute for war. There were no horse tracks about the ruins. The burning had happened a long time before. Everything was utterly silent. And he knew that he hadn't come home, after all, because there wasn't any home for him to come to.

He got off his horse, stunned. Presently he heard voices. He mounted—it did not occur to him to walk— and rode to the sound. It was Negroes, walking in single file through a field of shiftless, unhoed corn. He stared at them. They were strange Negroes. None of the old plantation hands. They huddled together when they saw him, white-faced and stricken, splendidly clad in a gray uniform and with a bright sword.

He asked questions. Politely. But sullen glances answered. Then a strident, insolent reply. They didn't know anything about any house here. The house was burned down before they came. The Freedman's Bureau had sent them here, with forty acres to a family, because this land was taken up for taxes and distributed to freedmen by the white gentlemen from the North. He better go ask questions at the Freedman's Bureau in town. . . .

It was hopeless to get more out of them. They bunched together. The women slipped away through the cornstalks. The men were scared but sullen. He could have driven them before him like sheep. But it would have been useless, because all things were changed. He turned and rode away. He never saw his birthplace again.

It was hours, though, before he found anyone who would or could tell him what he needed to know. At long last, five miles from his own plantation, he found the gray-haired former judge of the circuit court, now in patched overalls and doggedly hoeing a melon patch. There was nothing better for him to do, since he had served the Confederacy. He was disfranchised and reduced to a state of second-class citizenship far below his own freed slaves.

The judge gave Blayde water to drink and offered him hoecake to eat. Reluctantly he told the young man that his family was dead. A gang of bushwhackers—they'd called themselves guerrillas during the war—had ridden through the county, plundering and looting. There was no force to oppose them. The Yankees were not too much concerned about anybody preying on former enemies of the United States. The bushwhackers—bandits, outlaws— had shot down Blayde's father on his own front porch and had shot down his mother in the entrance hall as she ran toward her husband. They'd looted the house and left it burning when they went away.

Young Blayde Hollister said in a queer voice that he'd
had a sister too.

That was not so easy for a former judge and adminis-
trator of justice to tell about. The judge said that it was
the Marlow brothers' gang that had done the looting
and killing. They'd gone on somewhere, down toward
Alabama.

Colonel Blayde Hollister, aged twenty-two, repeated
that he'd had a sister. His voice rose a little in pitch.
It grew strained and harsh.

The judge hesitated, and then said in a shamed voice
that she was dead, too. She hadn't been killed at the
house. One of the Marlow brothers—it was Bryant—had
carried her off. But at the camp of the bushwhackers
that same night she'd managed to get hold of a revolver,
and she'd opened fire with it, and she'd killed one man
and wounded another before Bryant shot her dead. A
darky who'd been hanging around the bandit camp told
about it afterward. Her body'd been brought back. She
was buried with her parents.

This was told to Blayde Hollister in the bright sunshine of a Georgia morning, when he'd come home to
help his family face the future that must follow the ending of the world they'd known.

Two hours later he was in town, with his eyes deep-
sunk and his face a marble white. He went to the Freedman's Bureau and asked in a sort of still calmness for
news of his plantation. It had been looted and burned
and then, he was told, taken over for taxes.

A sandy-haired and freckled Yankee, a political ap-
pointee to the noble work, looked condescendingly into
the records. He said that the plantation had been abandoned, so it had been sequestered and divided among
freedmen. And, he added gratuitously, it wa'n't likely
that any damn rebel would have any attention paid to
him if he complained.

Blayde Hollister said politely that his actual concern
was with the Marlow gang, which had burned his house
and murdered his parents and sister.

The Freedman's Bureau referred him scornfully to the military authorities.

He went to the office of the commandant of the town. There was a gangling, rawboned sentry outside. He blinked at the moderately resplendent uniform worn by Blayde. He could not very well shoot—the war was over —but he did not know what else to do. He gaped. He was one of the occupation troops recruited to hold down and suitably subdue the South.

Blayde went grimly into the commandant's office. It smelled of whisky and stale tobacco. There was a Federal captain sitting at a desk, counting out a pile of greenbacks into a tin box. It could be Army pay money or almost anything else. Young Colonel Blayde Hollister, C.S.A., halted just inside the door. The Federal captain looked up with a start.

"My name," said Blayde steadily, "is Hollister. It appears that my family has been murdered and my home looted and burned by a gang of bushwhackers headed by the Marlow brothers. The murder and looting took place well over a month ago. I would like to know if there is any recent news of that gang."

The Federal captain closed his mouth, which had dropped open. He shut the tin box with the money in it. He thrust it hastily into a drawer of his desk. His face turned red.

He eyed the insignia on Blayde's collar. He felt the resentment an older captain feels for a younger colonel. Added to it was the scorn of a victor—some victors—for the vanquished. He looked Blayde Hollister up and down.

"A colonel, eh? A reb colonel! Coming to ask help against some other rebs, eh?"

"Not help," said Blayde Hollister very quietly. "If they've been caught and hanged I will make myself satisfied. But I would like to know if they are still alive."

The Federal captain said violently, "You're wearing a complete rebel uniform! You're wearing a sword and pistol! That's a violation of your parole! Let me see your military pass!"

Blayde said, "I have no pass. I've given no parole. I disbanded by regiment and came home, to find my family murdered and my house burned down. I'm asking if the murderers have by any chance been caught—not that you and you kind bothered them while they were here!"

The Federal captain turned redder. "You damn rebs! You've got no right to ask anything of the United States government under any conditions! You're under arrest! You'll find that you can't dodge the laws about rebels who try to defy the government. Sneaking about back roads—conspiring, for all I know—"

He stood up and held out his hand imperiously. "Your sword and pistol! You go to jail while we look into your record! By God, we'll teach you rebels—"

In justice to the Federal captain, it must be recorded that he had served in the office of the provost marshal in Washington all during the four years of fighting. He had done no soldiering at all himself, and he had read vast quantities of inflammatory literature designed to spur the patriotism of the North. So he was much more inflamed against the South and all its people than an actual fighting soldier would have been. His whole mental processes were unlike those of a soldier who had shot at Confederates and dodged their bullets. He proved it when he advanced upon Blayde in his own office, raging, without even the elementary precaution of drawing a weapon of his own.

He was shocked to discover himself looking into a Confederate Army revolver, held in a steady hand. Blazing eyes looked into his.

"I'll trouble you," said Blayde coldly, "to tell me about the Marlow brothers. Have they to your knowledge been captured or traced since they left these parts?"

The Federal captain quieted instantly. Any man would. He said in a much moderated tone, "I've had no word of them. They went on south from here. That's all I know."

"Very well," said Blayde. "I've given no parole. But will you give me yours to raise no alarm while I leave?"

But the captain had recovered his nerve. "I will not!"

he snapped. "You'll be caught and hanged for this! The sentry outside—"

He opened his mouth to call furiously. He had been only momentarily overawed by the weapon. He was not a coward. He was merely an obstinate and opinionated civilian in uniform.

A Confederate gun barrel crashed against his skull. He collapsed. By coincidence he fell neatly back into his chair.

Blayde regarded him coldly. Then he called authoritatively, "Sentry!"

The sentry came in, slouching a little. Occupation duty did not appeal to men who had fought for four years. They wanted to go home. So the occupation forces were largely very fresh troops. The sentry gasped when he found a heavy Colt pressed against his belly with its hammer at full cock.

"Your captain," said young Colonel Hollister icily, "is not able to listen. You will report to him that since he insisted on resuming hostilities, I am acting as a soldier. Lean your musket against the wall."

He watched as the sentry obeyed. He took a slip of paper from the captain's desk and wrote on it with fine precision:

> I acknowledge the receipt of one tin box containing currency, requisitioned by me.
>   BLAYDE HOLLISTER
>   Colonel
>   Fifth Georgia Cavalry
>   C.S.A.

He disabled the sentry's rifle, opened the desk drawer, and tucked the tin box under his arm. He took the Federal captain's pistol and stuck it in his belt.

"I would say that he has ignored a very definite duty to keep his district clear of bandits under arms," he told the sentry frostily, "and his excuse is that as far as I am concerned the war is not ended. I am taking him at his word and taking up the work that he should have done. I have requisitioned"—he smiled very grimly—"supplies for the task. I am leaving now. Perhaps I should remind you that in guerrilla action it is always the practice for someone to stay behind and shoot the first man to give an alarm."

He went out and mounted, with the tin box under his arm. He rode away. He was three hundred yards down the highway before the first scared yell came from the sentry's throat. Long before anything like effective measures could be taken to capture him, he was clear of the town. He turned aside from the highway and rode into the woods.

At that time he had no idea of ever going to Texas. It was a logical place for a man to hide himself in, of course, whether he wished to leave behind a past that was murderous or merely indiscreet. And he knew that from this instant he would be on the list of very special offenders against the peace and dignity of the United States. There was no oblivion for people on that list. Washington was victorious over Richmond, and it was politic merely to grind down and humiliate but not otherwise punish those who had served and fought for the Confederacy. It was even politic to be condescendingly admiring of some of the Confederate generals. But individuals charged with crimes not allowable in war, and those others who were not protected by their eminence and were so presumptuous as to refuse to grovel—for them there was no forbearance. Colonel Blayde Hollister would now be added to their number. He would be one with Jefferson Davis and his cabinet, the captains of the Confederate naval raiders, and those sadists who had enjoyed their opportunities for cruelty as guards over prisoners of war.

There would be posters printed denouncing him. As soon as they were distributed, he would be hunted everywhere. But those posters would also, automatically, provide him with some friends.

So Colonel Blayde Hollister rode through a pitch-pine

forest with a Yankee military payroll under his arm, as a part of preparations for a mission assigned him by fate. There is always a need for the punishment of crime by individuals, when a government refuses to carry out its obligation to protect its people.

He thought he might be able to run down and settle with the Marlow brothers within weeks. Then, if the Yankees wished it, he could ride in and politely submit himself to what they were pleased to call justice. But he must find the gang that had murdered his parents and sister. In particular—oh, most especially!—he must kill that Marlow brother named Bryant, who had carried his sister off and who later had shot her dead.

In pursuit of that objective, the young man in the neatly brushed gray uniform rode south. As he rode he reflected coldly that he must stop wearing this uniform and sword. On his present mission, by the rules of war the rules of war did not apply. As in the capture of a New England village by a raiding party of Confederates striking from Canada, and the incendiary attack on New York that was so complete a failure, Blayde would have to resort to unmilitary measures to achieve an end the military forces should have accomplished.

He did not think it would take more than a few weeks. But he was a long way off in his estimate.

Chapter Two

IT WAS AN honest Yankee officer in Alabama—there were such—who spoiled Blayde's chances of catching the Marlows right away. The Yankee officer was much disliked by the fresh-raised occupation troops under his command. For example, when he heard of a bushwhacker gang headed down through Georgia, he took measures. His men cursed him, but he'd never liked looters and murderers even in wartime, when they called themselves guerrillas. He didn't like them any better now that the war was over.

He prepared for the coming of the Marlow gang. Blue-clad, fresh-raised volunteers, who had enlisted for a happy period of loafing in a conquered country, found themselves marching through thick woods and down muddy byways. He camped them in uncomfortable places and he had lines of pickets and mounted patrols in mosquito-infested spots. There were sore feet and fatigued muscles. The occupation troops were much annoyed.

Then the Marlow gang moved into Alabama, and instantly ran into waiting soldiers who already hated them cordially for having been the cause of all their exertions. The blue-clad soldiers fought inexpertly, but with venom. The bushwhackers lost four men in the first encounter, and had no loot to show for it. There were two other skirmishes. Then they seemed to elude the soldiers. They congratulated themselves. They sent a messenger to a kinsman of one of their number and prepared to prosper and enjoy life again. But their messenger came back with his eyes popping out. He reported that soldiers were moving up all around them. They were already hemmed in. He could almost feel a noose already about his neck.

It was no time to fight, and it was too late to run. So the bushwhackers took the only other course left open to them. They evaporated. In units of two and three men, sweating and terrified, they scattered and set out to filter through the trap that had been closing in about them. Most of them got away. Two men only were actually caught, and they desperately tried to fight and then very foolishly surrendered. They were hanged expeditiously by the order of the honest Yankee officer, who was later removed from his post in consequence of his honesty in another matter entirely. But the Marlow brothers' gang had ceased to be. It would never gather again in its full strength.

That was the situation Blayde found when he followed the two-month-old trail of his family's murderers into Alabama. He was no longer wearing Confederate gray then. There were posters up, commanding all men to search for one Blayde Hollister, late colonel in the Confederate Army, who had continued guerrilla action after the cessation of hostilities. The posters were not too unjust. They contained a reasonably accurate account of his having requisitioned a military payroll and left a receipt for it. The action of receipting somehow kept the action, even in Yankee minds, from seeming mere armed robbery. But unfortunately it made it treasonable armed warfare against the United States, which was a capital offense again now that Lee and Johnston had surrendered.

The poster, however, also made friends for Blayde. Men who had themselves surrendered—and would do so again under the circumstances—felt a rueful admiration for a man who had not. They would not have helped a bandit, but they would help a man carrying on the rebellion in which they had failed. So the name of "Reb" Hollister came into being, and many people wished him well. But none could help him to find the Marlows. There was absolutely nothing to indicate whether they still hid out in Alabama or had gone on to other fields. They could have hidden. They had kinfolk in the region. They could have gone to Texas, of course. Or they might have gone only to Missouri, which was hardly law-abiding country yet, or they might be heading for the Far West.

Blayde searched diligently for some sort of trail to follow, while the name of "Reb" Hollister became more familiar than his own. A hunt at random would be hopeless. In the end he took a leaf from the Yankee notebook. He had a country printer run off posters of his own design. He posted them in likely places, and it became a commonplace in parts of Alabama to find two separate proclamations side by side. One would be a formal notice from the military government that ruled Georgia and Alabama together, with General Meade in command. That poster read:

WANTED
Blayde Hollister
Late Colonel, Confederate Army
for
Criminal Guerrilla Action Against
The United States Army
After the Cessation of Legal Hostilities.

There followed a statement of his offense as it appeared to the military authorities, with a description of his person.

The poster next to it was often Blayde's:

$5,000 REWARD IN U. S. GREENBACKS
for information guiding the undersigned to the present whereabouts of the Marlow brothers, who were bushwhackers and guerrillas during the late war, and have lately looted, murdered, and burned in Georgia and other places. Their gang being now dispersed and the Marlow brothers being fugitives, the undersigned will pay $5,000 in U. S. greenbacks to anyone guiding or directing him to their hiding place.

BLAYDE HOLLISTER
Colonel, C.S.A.

His poster stirred up a hornet's nest. The honest Yankee officer who had scattered the gang might have been amused or sympathetic. But his successors were enraged. The occupation troops were stirred up to a furious zeal. Former Confederates grinned—they had little else to grin about—and joyously kept him informed of the hunt for him. But the friends and kinfolk of the Marlows were concerned. Of course, most of them would have sold out their relatives for a fraction of the price Blayde offered, but they couldn't. So as a next best thing, one of them informed upon him.

It was a narrow escape, but Blayde got away by riding hard and fast through unfamiliar forest, guided by the moonlight speckles that filtered through the leaves. Three times he exchanged pistol shots with those who would have seized him. But it was time for him to move on, anyhow. That part of Alabama had become much too hot for those who befriended him, and it was clear that the fault in the trail of the Marlows was absolute. There was no longer a trail.

He had learned a little about them, but not much. There were three brothers. Their mother, poor woman, had named them for a great poet, aspiring pathetically on their behalf for better things than her own life had known. The oldest was William, the second Cullen, and the third Bryant. The trace of poetic sensibility in their mother, however, had not affected the sons. They had been known as criminals and troublemakers even before the war. They had earned an unsavory reputation with Quantrell during hostilities. And afterward, the crime for which Blayde trailed them was only one of many. But he kept it distinctly in his mind that though all of them were guilty, it was Bryant who had carried off his sister, and Bryant who had shot her dead.

Now all three were vanished as if the earth had swallowed them. At that time, though, there were two most likely places for them to have gone: Missouri, where the Marlows had kinsmen, and Texas, where others of their kind had gone before.

So Blayde rode to Missouri and began his hunt again. He took a supply of his posters with him. They were still more likely to produce results than mere random searching of his own. Presently they appeared in minor hamlets and sizable towns all through the state. They made men talk. About the Marlow brothers. If anybody knew anything about them, it would not long remain a secret. Blayde's quest became the subject of gossip everywhere. "If you want five thousand Yankee dollars," the word spread, "all you got to do is tell Reb Hollister where the Marlows are. Ever heard of 'em?"

And it was not necessary to give an address at which Blayde could be found, either. If somebody wanted to find him, the word would get about and a meeting could be arranged. There was no occupation government in Missouri. There had been a minor rebellion against its Secessionist governor, and Missouri stayed in the Union. So quite half its population was now complacent.

There was just one point that didn't occur to the young man who had been Colonel Blayde Hollister of the Fifth Georgia Cavalry. He could see how his offer of a reward in U. S. money for the whereabouts of other outlaws—himself being an outlaw—would affect the public. The irreverent would be amused, and the Confederates would be pleased. He could also see how it would affect the military and all Federal officers everywhere. It would be like waving a red flag before a bull.

But he didn't see how it would affect the Marlow brothers. They were bound to hear of it. They were bound to react to it. They were bound to do something about it. And he did not anticipate the fact.

He had, for a time, some worry about his personal affairs. Five thousand dollars had to be kept intact to pay out as reward if it should be claimed. And he had to eat, and he had to buy forage for his horse, Yank.

Yank provided the answer in himself. Yank was a big, black animal found wandering scared and riderless after a skirmish near Morgan Springs. He was an officer's horse; certainly he was no supply-service-purchased mount. His

owner was dead, so Blayde took the big animal as a prize
of war and rode him thereafter. He named him Yank
and considered the title appropriate, because Yank was
a good deal more capable than he at first appeared.

He was a big-boned horse, and heavily built, but he
had a surprising turn of speed. Blayde entered him in a
race in a small Mississippi town and bet most of his
available cash on him. He won. Moving on, making his
inquiries and putting up his posters, he raced the big
horse again and again. Before long Yank became almost
too famous. Blayde bought another saddle horse. A
stunted, tobacco-chewing Negro attached himself to the
two animals. Then Blayde traveled in state.

But he learned nothing of the Marlows. Once he
thought he'd found them under another name. He traveled to the very northern border of Missouri. But the
brothers he came upon were named James. He inter-
viewed them courteously. They had heard of him and
they knew the Marlows, but they had not seen Blayde's
quarry since both family groups had raided with Quantrell. The James boys were already acquiring an unpleasant fame as robbers. Himself outlawed, the former
Colonel Hollister could hardly criticize. Themselves former Confederates—of a sort—the James boys could not
well try to murder Blayde without some excuse. Perhaps
they thought it unwise to try, anyhow. Blayde parted
from them politely, but without warmth.

Another set of brothers drew him far into Kansas.
They were the Younger brothers, then only coming into
prominence as bank robbers. But they were not the Marlows, either. He went back to Missouri in hope that his
publicity campaign might have borne some fruit. He
was now famous. Absolutely everybody entering the state
of Missouri would sooner or later hear of the famous
unreconstructed Reb Hollister, who hadn't surrendered
to the Yankees and offered five thousand Yankee dollars
for news of some men he was hunting.

It was in Sassafras, Missouri, that he had the first real
reason to hope for success in his wearisome search. Sassa-

fras was a very small settlement indeed; a straggling line
of log and sod shacks along the muddy river's edge, with
a few slatternly, subdued women in the smaller shacks,
and two stores that sold atrocious whisky by the gallon.
And there was a hotel. Of sorts. Very much of sorts.

He put up at the hotel. There was to be horse racing
next day at Greenville, a few miles on. The Negro boy
who had attached himself to Blayde's fortunes slept in
the stable with the two horses. Blayde retired early. For
the purpose to which he had devoted himself, a certain
amount of geniality was needful. But he could not find
any satisfaction in backwoods revelry in the forms it took
after nightfall.

He slept soundly that night. The river flowed by. It
made gurgling sounds against the shore. There was music
somewhere in the settlement. Once there was a fight, with
loud oaths and crashing noises. Later a shotgun boomed
in the dark. Toward morning silence fell, save for the
murmuring of the nearby trees.

Not long after sunrise, Blayde waked. Outside there
was the deep, deep stillness of a Missouri settlement when
all its inhabitants slept the heavy sleep of morning. Only
the river murmured. There was not even the cackling of
a hen or a rooster's crow to break the stillness. Blayde
got up, went to the window, and looked out over the
river. The trees on the farther shore were a darker green
than trees should be. The sky was hardly graying. Thin
streaks of cloud floated low on the horizon. They were
pink. The rest of the world was dark, dark green, and
gray, and the sullen heavy yellow of the river. There were
wisps of foggy mist floating on the water.

Blayde put his head out of the window to smell the
morning air, to take great gulps of it.

There was a raucous, bellowing explosion. Instantly
there was another. The glass immediately above his head
flew to splinters and fell tinkling to the floor behind him.

His pistol leaped into his hand—afterward he had no
memory of having drawn it—and he poured lead at a
spot where a white cloud of powder smoke had sprung

into being beside the corner of a log house. An instant later he had snatched up another weapon and was out the window and running toward the spot.

When he reached it, there were only heelprints in the muddy ground; that, and hoofbeats going off into the distance at a panic-stricken rate. There was no other sign of the man who had tried to kill him.

But Blayde grinned as he went back to the unspeakable shack that passed for a hotel. He made himself ready for the road. He even hummed a bit. He was encouraged. This was the first sign he'd had that the Marlow brothers were still alive. He hadn't looked for it, but he recognized it for what it was. Somebody had tried to kill him from a distance that ruled out robbery as motive. And the Marlow brothers were the only people on earth with anything to gain by his death. They would feel safer. They had heard of his reward offer. They had sent somebody to kill him.

He left the settlement early, with the tobacco-chewing, stunted Negro youth riding behind him. Half a mile out of Sassafras, Blayde said:

"Somebody talked to you, Jode, last night after I had gone to bed."

"Yessuh," said Jode, wide-eyed. "A gentleman said he admired you right much, suh."

"He asked you all sorts of things about me?" asked Blayde without heat. He drew comfortably on a long, thin cigar.

"Yessuh. Even how you slep', suh, an' what time you riz up, suh, an' what time a gen'leman could git a fust look at you in the mornin', suh. Said you was a great man, suh, and he'd admire to see you even from a distance, suh."

Blayde considered. "So you told him about my liking to take a look at the weather first thing when I wake, eh?" he asked dryly.

"Yessuh."

"I hope he tipped you well."

"He gimme a quarter, suh," said Jode.

"He emptied a double-barreled shotgun at me when

I looked at the weather, Jode. What did he look like?"

Jode told him, distressed. Blayde frowned. The boy was honestly upset. He told the truth. But the description did not fit any of the three Marlow brothers as they'd been described to Blayde. It was a description that had no special features about it. It would fit hundreds of backwoodsmen. He shook his head.

"Tell me if you ever see him again," he commanded. "It looks like he was a friend of the men I'm after. Too bad. They must be a long way off. Did you see his horse?"

"I ain't sure which one was his'n, suh. There was four-five hawsses in the hotel stable besides ourn."

Blayde shook his head regretfully. He rode on. But he watched the trail ahead. So early in the morning there was just one set of hoofprints in the dew-damp ground. And this was the road on which his would-be assassin had sped away. The track might mean something, but of course it might not. Blayde rode at ease, keeping an eye on the trail. Presently it became merged with the hoof-marks of other animals. He overtook some of the other riders, but Jode shook his head as each was overtaken. No horse was familiar, nor did he recognize the riders. They were whiskery, hard-bitten characters of the backwoods. Some rode for Blayde's own destination, Greenville. He made no secret of his identity and gathered what information he could. It was not much.

At a roadside store he saw the particular trail again. He couldn't have told what was particular about it, any more than he could have described another man's nose. But he recognized it. He asked in the store. Yes, a man had ridden by a little while ago on a brown horse with a brand on it. A Texas horse. He hadn't paused. His description fitted Jode's. He was, as a ten-to-one probability, the man who had shot at Blayde. But it was still only an odds-on likelihood. Blayde rode on, meditating carefully.

He reached Greenville at noon. It might have owned a hundred inhabitants, but already fully four hundred men were gathered for the races. There were very few women in sight, and they were of the pathetically blowzy type of the backwoods siren. The women of the settlement stayed indoors, which was wise. But Blayde saw their suspicious eyes peering from windows and cracked-open doors. From certain individuals in the crowd, however, he received a cordial welcome. Former Confederates greeted him with cautious warmth. One man, though, said earnestly:

"Colonel, you want to watch out heah. This was a nest o' Unionists durin' the war. They hid run-off slaves an' helped the Yankees all they could. They ain't honest folks, Colonel."

"All I want here," said Blayde, "is to win a little money racing and"—he added it casually—"find a man on a Texas horse. He shot at me this morning."

"Don't know him, suh," said his informant, "but you watch out, Colonel. Ain't many of us Confeds around. I wouldn't be heah myself, but a man's got to have some fun sometimes."

The preparations for festivity consisted of a rope corral where the horses were to be raced, a course laid out between two lines of stakes with rags on their ends, and two wagons dispensing snakehead whisky from their tailboards. The price was two cents for a small drink, five cents a cupful, or thirty cents a quart—which was exorbitant in view of its quality.

Blayde tethered his two horses to picket pins and mingled with the crowd. In the course of two hours he found only half a dozen men who did not seem to regard him with great respect because of his notoriety. Mostly, he was greeted as a man of distinction. More, his horse was known and respected. But that was no reason to be less than careful.

The entrepreneurs of the race meet sought him out, beaming. They were a committee of six whiskered gentlemen who regarded him with seeming fondness while they poisoned the air about them. They explained that there was just one horse at the meet that might have a chance of beating his big horse, Yank. They had been

circulating among the crowd to gather a bet worthy of
his attention. In honor of his distinction and fame, they
were prepared to bet five hundred dollars in greenbacks,
even money, on the local mare, the race to be run a full
mile between the line of rag-tipped stakes, breaking from
the track to be a forfeit, and the race to be one heat.

"A very sporting offer, gentlemen," said Blayde politely.
"You don't mind if my darky Jode rides jockey, do you?"

They did not mind. They went with him to the spot
where the big horse nibbled at the grass about his picket
pin. Jode came into sight as they regarded Yank blandly.
His eyes were excited and uneasy. Blayde told him to
prepare for the race. Jode looked almost appealing, as
if he wanted very badly to say something, but there was
no chance for a private word.

The committee praised Yank fulsomely and accompanied him to the starting point. A very well-built little
mare was already waiting there. She was neglected and
nervous, but there was good blood in her lines, and she
was certainly stolen. So good a horse would not arrive
honestly in the back settlements. Blayde, though, was
hardly in a position to be censorious. He counted out
five hundred dollars into the hand of a whiskered, villain-
ous-seeming person who by description would have passed
as cousin to all the crowd. The committee doled out five
hundred more to cover it, in dirty, worn, ragged bills evidently contributed from many pockets.

"We made up this bet in the crowd," said the head
of the committee, beaming, "so's it would be worthy of
a gentleman like yourself comin' to our race meetin',
suh. I reckon there's fifty-sixty men in this crowd that'll
be braggin' they once laid a bet against Colonel Reb
Hollister, suh!"

Blayde saw the point. Fifty or sixty men were betting
against Yank. This had been a nest of Unionists, like
half of Missouri.

The committeeman went on unctuously, "Yes, suh!
We're all right proud, suh, to have you heah. These two
gen'lemen will jedge the race, suh. The understandin'

is that it's one heat, an' breakin' out of the marked track
is a forfeit. Right, suh?"

"That's right," agreed Blayde formally.

He stood back. He cast his eyes quickly about. Four
hundred men in the crowd, a sizable fraction of them
standing to win if Yank lost. A tradition of Unionism,
which made a Confederate already half an enemy, though
the war was over. He had been maneuvered into a situation that could be awkward. But the track was clear.
It was uneven, but no worse than many Yank had raced
on, and it was plainly marked a half mile out and a
turn and a half mile back. There would be only the two
horses running. Most foul tactics would be patently impossible.

He moved to the horse's side and said curtly, "Jode,
keep clear of that other horse. Don't crowd her. Understand?"

"Yessuh," said Jode. He added in a low tone, "Colonel,
suh—"

"Later," said Blayde.

He stood back and waved his hand. A nervously grinning white boy bestrode the mare. The two horses made
ready. A man with piebald whiskers raised a pistol above
his head.

"Git ready!" he cried shrilly. "I'm agoin' to let her go!"

The jockeys tensed. The gun exploded. The horses
flung into headlong motion.

Tumult arose in the clearing that was the town of
Greenville. With so many concerned in the owners' stake,
all other activity had ceased. Even the whisky wagons
were without customers for the time being, though many
patrons had forehandedly provided themselves with tin
cups of beverage with which to refresh themselves during
the race. The two horses darted into the distance with
a stirring, shuddery thunder of racing hoofs. There is
nothing more beautiful than a running horse. These two
were magnificent.

Even Blayde almost forgot all other matters in the
watching of the race. Almost. Yells and howls arose as

the animals passed the quarter mark. At the half mile, Yank was half a length ahead. Blayde would have watched that only, except for an acquired and now habitual caution. Men flung tattered hats into the air. A man let off his shotgun. Other guns went off.

Blayde's hand fell to his hip and closed on the butt of his army Colt. He swept his eyes quickly about. He saw backs. All men watched the race—but one. One pair of eyes watched Blayde. But they vanished behind the shoulders and heads of howling, half-drunken men. There was a movement as of someone forcing his way violently through the crowd.

Blayde turned back toward the horse race. Yank was a length ahead now. Two lengths. He came down the home stretch, flinging his forehoofs splendidly, snorting in triumph. He was a hundred yards from the crowd that lined the course up to the finish line.

A man leaped in his path. A great red blanket flapped almost in the big animal's face. It swirled widely, wildly. It was terrifying.

Yank broke stride and reared to dodge the apparition. Then he swerved, his eyes rolling, as the man seemed to dart at him with the flailing blanket. Yank plunged out of the line of stakes, and the man lost himself in the crowd.

The mare came home, her jockey flogging her mercilessly, though Yank had plainly been fouled.

There was thunderous yelling. Guns exploded in an ecstasy of rejoicing. Half-drunken men pounded each other, howling with laughter. There were shrill screeches of triumph. Faces turned upon Blayde, red with mirth, alight with mocking laughter, split with wide, derisive grins.

He went utterly white. For seconds he stood almost rigid. The committee that had contrived the race now grinned at him like the rest of the crowd nearby.

" 'Twas agreed," said the chief committeeman, smirking, "that breakin' outa the marked course was a forfeit. You lose, suh!"

"My horse was fouled," said Blayde. His voice shook a
little. It was anger, but the committeemen did not read
it that way.

"I didn't see nothing," said the stake holder, giggling.

"Theah's fifty-sixty men in this crowd," said the head
of the committee complacently, "that'll agree theah
wa'n't nothin' irregular. Theah ain't nothin' you can do,
Mr. Reb Hollister!"

Then his mouth dropped open. Very suddenly, very
abruptly, he saw the true meaning of Blayde's immobility. There was pandemonium all about; shouts and shots
and exulting and derisive howlings. But the committeeman suddenly saw that Blayde was not overawed, and
that he was killing mad. In the middle of a mob rejoicing
over his defeat, of course he could be shot down with no
possibility of his killer's ever being called to account. But
Blayde threw back his coat deliberately. The chief committeeman reached for a pistol, fast. But he did not even
have time to turn pale.

Blayde's pistol came out first. He fired first. The other
weapons of the other committeemen were coming out
too—raggedly enough, but plainly by previous agreement; it was plainly prearranged. Blayde was known to
be ready to pay five thousand dollars in cash on receipt
of certain information. The committeemen jerked at
their weapons—ultimately to get that five thousand dollars—in the midst of a clamorous exultation. But Blayde's
Colt roared and roared again, and he sprang forward and
snatched at the stake holder's body as other weapons exploded, and he fired again and again, and was thrusting
ruthlessly through the rejoicing mob before anybody
realized that the drumfire of shots was not rejoicing.

He fired only once more, from his second pistol, before
he reached his picketed second horse. He jerked loose the
tether and swung into the saddle. Even then the word
was only beginning to spread through the crowd, and
then men pressed stupidly to see what had happened
rather than turning to look for Blayde.

He spurred in a circle around the crowd's edge. It was

wise, if not intentionally so, because a man fleeing from the scene of a shooting will be noted even by the drunk or dazed. But Blayde was plainly not fleeing.

He reached Jode, still fighting the big horse Yank. Blayde switched mounts. Yank calmed immediately.

"Come along," commanded Blayde, and shepherded Jode ahead of him into the nearest woods trail.

It was as the trees closed in behind them that the yelling of the crowd about the finish line died down abruptly, and the sounds of rejoicing turned to a buzzing noise of shock and argument and agitation.

"Suh," said Jode uneasily, "the gen'leman that axed questions about you las' night was the gen'leman that held the money on the race."

"Which I collected," said Blayde. "Too bad we can't ask questions of him now. Take it easy, Jode. If I'd downed one man they might be coming after us. But I think I picked off enough of them to be discouraging."

The stake holder had been the second man to be shot. He was dead. Blayde shrugged ruefully, but Jode said:

"Suh, I saw his hawss, too. It was a Texas hawss, suh, with a brand on him. Somebody'd branded him with a square an' a round, suh."

Blayde Hollister jerked his head to the small Negro.

"If you draw that brand for me, Jode," he said, "I'll pay you a hundred Yankee dollars. Think you can?"

"Yes, suh!" said Jode.

Blayde dismounted, ignoring the possibility of pursuit, and smoothed a clear place in the dirt. Jode squatted down and absorbedly traced a square and a circle in the earth. Blayde looked at it intently. He didn't know that it would be read Box O in Texas, but he did know that a friend of the Marlows, who had tried to kill him, had at some time been near a ranch that used that brand, if only to steal the horse that bore it.

It was not a clear trail to the Marlows, but it was the best clue Blayde had had since their disappearance.

That was when Blayde Hollister, colonel in the late Confederate Army, made up his mind to go to Texas.

Chapter Three

BLAYDE arrived in Springfield, Missouri, some time after dark. To a man who had seen only small towns and backwoods settlements for a long, long time, it was a brilliant sight. Turpentine lanterns flared brightly in the streets. Saloons and dance halls ran full blast, and the gambling houses were brightly glowing with the rock-oil lamps inside. There were many horses in the streets, and bullock-drawn wagons creaking in even as late as this with bales of hides and buffalo skins, and there were restless, zestful men everywhere, already wearing the distinctive costume of the cowboy. Springfield shared with Kansas City, now, the high honor of being a hide-and-cattle town and a gateway to the West. Money circulated freely.

Blayde rode down the main street with Jode behind him. It was a very glamorous sight indeed. Tonight the street was deep in dust instead of mud, and horses kept it stirred up so that a sort of golden faery mist appeared to hang in the air, what with lamplight shining on it. There was a piano banging in a dance hall, and tinny fiddles with it. There was a roaring chorus in a saloon, and somewhere down the street two men fought with their fists, bellowing at each other, and somewhere else a brightly painted woman shrieked improbable abuse at a man who slunk away from her, and a bullock cart squeaked solemnly as it moved between the saloons and dance halls, which, with gambling places, outnumbered less garish places of business by four to one.

Jode said in a whisper, "Suh, you ain't goin' to stay in this town?"

"Not long," said Blayde. "But what's the matter? Don't you like it?"

"No, suh!" said Jode firmly. "I got a hundred dollars. I ain't sleepin' in no town like this with all that money!"

Blayde turned in at a livery stable. He put up the two horses. He had Jode carry his saddlebags to a hotel, where he got a room and ordered a St. Louis newspaper. The paper cost half a dollar here, but it was forthcoming. He dismissed Jode and went to a restaurant to eat, with the newspaper in his pocket.

There was communicable and unavoidable excitement in the very air of Springfield. After he had eaten, Blayde strolled down the street, tingling a little with the feel of lusty life around him. He was still not quite twenty-three years old. He had set himself a mission, and he meant to carry it out, but it was curiously satisfying to see something more than the half-dead towns of eastern Mississippi and Missouri. Here, already, something of a new and spacious way of living began to appear. Here Texas men—they had cattle herded outside the town to be split into bunches of two and three hundred and driven to the Mississippi River and the eastern seaboard —here Texas men swaggered with the pugnacious pride that had made it a truism that a Texas horse will always buck and a Texas man will always shoot.

Blayde wanted to see what the St. Louis paper had to say about the Greenville affair, but he postponed it for a sight of the festivities Springfield offered as its only reason for existence on the borders of the West.

He'd heard about the town, of course. It had fancy gamblers and fancy women and a degree of toughness that had led its self-appointed authorities to hire James B. Hickok—Wild Bill—to serve as town marshal, because no peace officer with less of an earned reputation could hope to live to collect his pay.

Once men surged swiftly out of a saloon and Blayde heard a flurry of shots, and then the shooting stopped and the men went back into the saloon again. A cowboy on a Texas horse rode down the street, standing upright in his saddle and emptying his six-shooters at the sky. It was evidently a celebration, but to Blayde it seemed pointless. So it appeared to the cowboy, too, because when his guns were empty he rather abashedly reined in, headed his horse toward a saloon, dismounted, and went inside.

There was loud talk everywhere, and two men wept sentimentally together, staggering from one place to another, and a pair of boots projected from an alleyway between two buildings, and all passers-by politely stepped over them. There was a sudden howl of wrath, and a man came scuttling out of nowhere and ran dodging across the street, and a whiskered man came lunging out after him and fumbled out a pistol, but the fugitive was out of sight and the whiskered man glared belligerently about and went back inside, where a woman sang shrilly to the sound of a guitar.

It was distinctly a change from the backwoods. Blayde regarded it with a pleased attention. He, of course, fitted well enough into the picture. He had long since exchanged his Confederate uniform for civilian garb consisting of a broadcloth frock coat, gray trousers tucked into his boots, immaculate white linen—Jode had turned out to be an admirable laundress—and a black slouch hat. It was noncommittal, and would pass without remark. He might be a gambler or a planter or a cattleman in town clothes. In any case, he now wore two pistols frankly but not ostentatiously under the coat, and his cartridge belt was evidence that he was not a dude.

He walked from one end of the festive town to the other, and strolled back. It was a new kind of civilization, but it was fascinating as a change. Presently he went into a saloon—the light would be better for reading than he was likely to find at the hotel—and took a seat at a table with a drink before him. He lighted a cigar and hunted through the newspaper for word of the affair in Greenville. On the third page he found it.

St. Louis—The notorious Reb Hollister showed up in Greenville last week. He entered his horse in a local race meet, attended by citizens of the locality, and bet heavily on the result. When his horse broke out of the marked track and forfeited, Hollister demanded the payment of his bets on the ground that

his horse was winning when it fouled. The legiti-
mate winners of his bets refusing to pay up, without
warning he drew a revolver and emptied it into the
crowd of sportsmen, murdering three citizens and
seriously injuring two others. He then rode away,
eluding a posse that instantly pursued him. This
notorious outlaw is believed to be heading south,
perhaps to practice his murderous tactics upon citizens of the Lone Star State.

There was no other comment. He shrugged his shoulders. It wasn't true, but he was used to that by this time.
At least, though, in view of the reward he'd offered for
news of the Marlow brothers, if one of them had been
present or killed the fact would have been mentioned.

He sipped at his drink with the paper open before him.
He noticed an incongruous figure at another table. He
regarded the man with idle interest. He was a short man
wearing a boiled shirt and other garments that did not
place him at all, in Blayde's experience. His coat had
a velvet collar and lapels. His cravat was beautifully tied.
His clothes were cut with a precision Blayde had not seen
since the war, and he stirred, and he was wearing shoes.
Not boots; shoes. He watched the people about him with
a curiously professional intentness, as if storing away
everything he saw in a strictly businesslike fashion. The
wearing of shoes alone pointed him out as an Easterner.
He was noticing everything, from the style of the hanging lamps to the clothes of the people about him. But
he was not concerned with their faces. Blayde could not
make him out.

He glanced at his paper. General Sheridan had left to
take command of United States troops moving against the
Western Indians. The river steamers *United States* and
America had collided on the Ohio River and burst into
flames. Only twenty-five of seventy-six passengers on one
boat had survived. One of them, however, was the famous
violinist Ole Bull, who had waded ashore from the burning steamers, carrying his violin over his head. Wading

ashore seemed to be a bit of common sense that had not occurred to other passengers. General Custer had captured a large number of hostiles at Black Kettle, Wyoming. The James brothers had held up a bank at Warsaw, Illinois. Fire Engine Number One, in New York, had had its boiler explode while attending a fire at 59 Bowery, just opposite the Old Bowery Theatre, and killed four people and injured twenty-three others. King Theodore of Abyssinia had been defeated by the British. . . .

There was a sudden bustle at the entrance to the saloon. Men moved quickly aside to make room. Blayde looked up. There was a sudden tension, instantly apparent, which could only have come from the entrance of the man now surveying the interior of the saloon through black, shoe-button eyes. The sudden silence was a tribute to an individual a little under middle height in the very bloom of frontier fashion; a Prince Albert coat, fawn-colored trousers pulled down over brilliantly polished boots, diamond shirt studs, and a dead-black sombrero. He was at that stage of drunkenness where a man is deadly. Pearl-handled pistols showed at his waist.

There was silence. The man nodded his head with a curious mechanical effect.

"Good evening, gentlemen," he said metallically. "If any of you do not know me, I am John Kelvin. I came to Springfield to see Mr. Hickok—Wild Bill Hickok, as he is known. He is a . . ." Without intonation he uttered monstrous things. "But he seems to be out of town tonight. So I am looking for his friends. Has he any friends here tonight?"

There was an uneasy shifting. Wild Bill Hickok had friends, no doubt, but none were showing. Kelvin stared about the saloon.

"I would hate to miss Mr. Hickok," he said with inhuman precision, "because I understand that he plans to leave Springfield, and I would like to keep him here. Permanently."

Again a pause. Blayde noticed that the incongruous man, the one with a velvet-collared coat and shoes in-

stead of boots, was regarding the bad man with an in-
tense, absorbed, note-taking interest quite out of the
ordinary. Kelvin noticed it also.

He moved with an almost gliding motion. He came
to a stop barely ten feet from Blayde, staring down at the
man with the velvet collar. Kelvin was pale and his eyes
were absolutely without expression. They seemed all
pupils, all black. He stood with an unnatural stillness.

"You look at me strangely," he said in that toneless,
lifeless, uncanny voice. "Are you a friend of that . . .
Hickok?"

The seated man said mildly, "I know him. I'm a theatrical man. I came out here to talk business with him.
We're business acquaintances."

"Then you are his friend. I am going to kill you. Draw
your pistol."

The Easterner went white. Then he said between his
teeth, "I have no pistol. To shoot me would be murder."

Kelvin looked at him with expressionless eyes for long
seconds, standing with wholly unnatural immobility before him.

"True. I will give you five minutes to arm yourself.
I will come back. And just in case you are afraid, I give
you reason to arm yourself."

He spat. He paused. He turned and walked out of the
door like a machine.

The Easterner struggled to his feet, mopping at his
face. He was shaken. He was dazed. But he glared about
him with suddenly raging eyes. He had to try twice to
speak.

"Where can I buy a pistol?" he demanded hoarsely.
"By God, I'll kill him!"

He was trembling, but Blayde approved of him. He
rose and said gently, "I advise you, sir, to go out the
back way. He is a known bad man. It is no disgrace to
avoid getting killed. It would be foolish to stand on your
pride, sir."

But the Easterner shook his head. He saw the guns in
Blayde's belt. He said tautly, "I stay. You have pistols.

If you can spare one of them, I will be glad to purchase—"

Blayde gave him his left-hand gun. He said quietly, "Have you ever been in a duel?" When the other man shook his head, Blayde said matter-of-factly, "He is the aggressor and he will go and have a drink or two and work himself up into an even more murderous mood. He will come in shooting. Now, you get this pistol cocked, but don't hurry. I advise you to put your forefinger along the cylinder—so—and pull the trigger with the middle finger. You will aim by instinct when you point your finger at him. Aim for the belly, a little low. And keep cool and take your time."

The Easterner looked at him queerly and opened his mouth as if to speak. Then he shook his head.

"Thank you," he said.

He sat down at the table again. He lifted his glass with his left hand and drank from it. The glass did not tremble.

The saloon remained very quiet. Blayde reseated himself. His chair was against the wall, fairly well out of the line of fire. He puffed meditatively on his cigar.

The door crashed open and the man Kelvin was framed in it. But only for a moment. He moved toward the Easterner in a sort of blazing fury. His pistol flashed before he was fully inside the saloon. He seemed to rush forward behind a cloud of flame and smoke and thunder. The Easterner, by contrast, sat almost perfectly still, wearing an expression of tense intentness. Kelvin was barely ten feet away when the Easterner pulled the trigger. With the same peculiar air of businesslike intentness, he cocked the weapon and fired a second shot. Then there was a strange, dead stillness. Then a cushioned noise. Kelvin crashed to the floor. The Easterner's first bullet had torn through his abdomen and smashed into his backbone. The second had pierced Kelvin's heart.

The Easterner finished his drink. He needed it. Then, desperately white, he returned Blayde's pistol to him.

"Thank you very much," he said unsteadily.

He went out of the saloon. Blayde put away his

weapon. He watched composedly as the dead man was carried out. He finished his drink. He went back to the hotel and went to bed.

He was at breakfast next morning when a large man with sweeping mustaches and a marshal's star on his coat stopped beside the table.

"Good morning," said the peace officer amiably. "You did a favor to a friend of mine last night." Then he stopped. "Hm . . . Reb Hollister? You're Colonel Reb Hollister, aren't you?"

"I am. And you are Marshal Hickok. How do you do?" Blayde said pleasantly, but his hand moved to his gun.

Wild Bill Hickok stroked one side of his mustache and grinned. "Colonel Hollister," he said reproachfully. "A friend of my friend is my friend; I have no intention of trying to arrest you, suh. If you will take your hand off your pistol, I would like to join you at breakfast and make your acquaintance, suh. It would be an honor."

Blayde stood up and bowed. It was not wholly a formal gesture. It showed that he had taken his hand away from his weapon. And Wild Bill bowed as profoundly and sat down opposite him and bellowed for service and for food in a fashion at once approving and grateful.

"To tell the truth, Colonel," he boomed, tucking a napkin into his vest, "you did me a great favor last night. Mr. Newell, who borrowed your pistol, is a theatrical manager. There is some talk of my treading the boards— I think that's the term—and he was here to arrange a contract with me."

Food came for both of them. It was breakfast. But this was Springfield, Missouri, and a gateway to the West. There was steak. There was coffee. There were wild turkey and prairie chicken and corn bread, for breakfast.

"I have a reputation," boomed the Marshal. "There is to be a play written about parts of my life. Mr. Newell will have the play written, he will see that the actors are suitable, and I am to tour the East with it. It should pay better than being town marshal"—Hickok grinned again—"and—well—I had made up my mind to go through with it. But if Mr. Newell had been killed last night while I was out of town, of course I'd have killed Kelvin, but my plans would have been sadly put awry."

"I see," said Blayde.

"I heard you were in town," confided Hickok, with exactly the air of a man telling a joke on himself, "and it occurred to me that—you are fairly famous, Colonel!— that you would be a very fitting climax to my career in Springfield. The newspapers, Mr. Newell tells me, would have made a great to-do had I encountered you this morning, and in a fight—oh, most reluctantly fought, you understand!"—Wild Bill twitched his eyebrows quizzically—"happened to kill you. On my last day of duty as a peace officer before taking to the stage, it would have been a very splendid thing."

Blayde carefully cut a bit off his steak and put it in his mouth. Wild Bill explained cheerfully:

"But when I met the little man, he told me you'd saved his life. Gave him good advice, lent him a pistol— and he's killed his man and likes it! My contract is signed, Newell is delighted with himself and with me, and—you are my friend, Colonel Hollister!"

"It is a great honor," said Blayde politely. "I am most fortunate not to be the climax of your career, Mr. Hickok."

Marshal Hickok chuckled. "I didn't mean to sound conceited, Colonel. But this morning my purpose is to offer you my friendship. You are hunting men I do not know. The Marlow brothers. I thought I knew most of the more notorious killers."

Blayde explained. Quantrell's raiders. Strictly local criminality before the war. More ambitious misdeeds after it. They had run into Union troops and had to scatter in order to escape.

"They murdered my father and mother and sister," added Blayde, giving no details. "They burned down my house. So I'm after them." He explained why he was in Springfield, on his way to Texas to hunt for a ranch with a brand of a square and a circle, because a presumed emissary of the Marlows, riding a horse of that brand, had tried twice to kill him. Twice. Once in Sassafras with a shotgun, and once in Greenville by organizing a combined swindle and murder.

Wild Bill ate hugely, listening. He was a distinctly flamboyant figure. He dominated any room he entered. He was accustomed to the awe of all beholders. Blayde treated him with cordial politeness, but without awe. And Wild Bill regarded him shrewdly, and matched his manner to Blayde's.

"I appreciate your position, Colonel," he said profoundly, when Blayde had finished. "I agree with your decision. But—I have seen a good many men turn killers. I have had to kill some of them. May I speak as your friend?"

Blayde waited. The restaurant was small and close. There was the smell of cookery in it. Its walls were rough planks, only sparsely decorated with pictures cut from the very occasional magazines to reach the frontier. Outside, hide wagons plodded by in seemingly endless procession, stirring up the powdery surface of the street into a dense, yellowish fog through which the horned oxen appeared dimly, moving their heads as oxen do when pulling. The dust swirled away and showed a wagon, and closed in again and hid it.

"A young man," said Wild Bill, leaning back to light a cigar, "often feels that he has nothing to live for."

Blayde suddenly realized that with seeming casualness Hickok had chosen a chair that put his back against a blank wall. Without appearing to do so, he had taken care during every single instant of their talk that he could not possibly be taken by surprise.

"It may be a girl," said Wild Bill impressively, "or a quarrel or a misfortune. Perhaps nothing more than getting drunk and sobering to find that one has killed someone. In your case, your world ended when the war did."

"There was my father," said Blayde.

"The war ended," said Wild Bill. "Some men had nothing to go back to. I've had to kill one or two of them. You

had something. Your family. But when you got back to it,
it was gone too. So you took up the pursuit of your parents' murderers. You again had something to live for.
Now, when you have punished the men who wiped out
your family, Colonel, what will you have?"

"I haven't thought," said Blayde.

"You will have nothing," Wild Bill told him. "As you
know, Colonel, I have some reputation. Because of it I
am leaving the scenes in which I gained it. And why? Because every braggart in the West knows that his boastings
of being a bad man are so much wind until he's stood up
to me. Every fool who tries to act the bully is foolish even
in his own mind until he has shot it out with me. To kill
me would set any man up in reputation." He spread out
his hands. "I do not boast. It is so. But it means that I
have already had to kill several men I had no desire to
kill. In this very city, only last night, I would have had
to kill John Kelvin had I been here."

Hide wagons creaked by outside. Then the tossing
horns of cattle appeared. Somebody or other was driving
a bunch of a hundred longhorns through the streets of
Springfield. Horsemen and the lank, gaunt figures of
range cattle appeared in the dust fog. Tossing horns
showed in the mistiness. Wild Bill did not even glance
out the window at them.

"That will be your fate, Colonel," said Hickok earnestly, "if you do not take care. You are already famous. Already it has occurred to some young fool that to be known
as the man who killed Reb Hollister would be a distinction. If you go to Texas and kill these Marlows, you will
still be an outlaw. You will be even better known than
you are now. You will have to live as I do, with two
pistols at your hips and"—here the town marshal of Springfield lowered his voice—"and derringers in your coat
pockets. I have told you a secret, there."

He grinned in a friendly fashion at Blayde.

"As your friend I point out that you head for great sad-
ness. When you have avenged your family, you should
have another purpose in mind. To one of your age, Col-

onel, I would suggest tranquillity. The West needs young
men with other purposes than the desire to have a reputa·
tion as a killer. You should marry and settle down."

Blayde put down his coffee cup. "I am going to find
the men who murdered my family," he said quietly. "That
is definite. After that, you tell me that I will be a target
for every fool who fancies himself a bad man. How will
I have a chance to settle down?"

Wild Bill grinned widely. There was a humorous sly-
ness in that grin.

"That is what I am coming to. A new United States
marshal is due in Springfield on this morning's stage. He
would be a splendid witness. I suggest, Colonel, that—"

He leaned forward and whispered. Blayde blinked at
him, startled.

"How's that?"

Hickok's voice dropped to a murmur. The small restaurant had no other customers. Wild Bill Hickok was not
safe company except in his most expansive moods. Few
ordinary people wanted to do more than greet him very
respectfully. Now he spoke at some length, his eyes at once
twinkling and shrewd, his manner at once humorous and
matter-of-fact. And his proposal, as he elaborated on it,
had a hard core of common sense, even though it was so
admirably suited to the purposes of one James B. Hickok
on the eve of a theatrical career.

Presently Blayde smiled faintly and then nodded in
agreement. There was a certain amount of detail to be settled. The stage coming through from St. Louis should
arrive somewhere near noon. There should be a brand-
new United States marshal on it, on his way to his proper
sphere of duty. There would doubtless be other passengers, so that the stage would carry on with it the story of
what would happen in consequence of this murmured
conference over a breakfast table. It would reach the
newspapers and undoubtedly would be transmitted both
to those effete Eastern cities whose gaslit theatres Wild
Bill was to adorn, and to Texas, where the Marlows or
their friends held sway.

When the town marshal swaggered off down the street, Blayde thoughtfully finished his cigar. Then he hunted up Jode. Jode had hidden out somewhere overnight, and he looked seedy. He had apparently heard tales intended to frighten a newcomer to these parts, and the tales had had their designed effect. He was scared.

Blayde was amused. Jode tried to look all ways at once, even when alone with Blayde in the stable connected with the livery corral.

"You look worried, Jode," said Blayde.

Jode looked at him and grimaced. "Colonel, suh, you paid me a hundred Yankee dollars. What am I goin' to do with 'em?"

Blayde waited. Jode said wretchedly:

"Suh, in this heah town theah's plenty men would kill anybody in the worl' for a hundred Yankee dollars. If somebody finds out I got that much, suh, how long is a colored boy like me goin' to live? Me, that ain't never shot off a gun in my life?"

"I see," said Blayde.

"If I stay heah, suh, I got to hide I got it. If I got to hide I got it, suh, what good is it to me? But do I go back to Nawth Ca'lina, suh, I'm rich. Heah, I'm just cold meat."

Blayde nodded. "You want to go home."

"Suh, I *got* to go home! I'll buy me a mule an' a gun an' a cook pot, suh, an' build me a cabin an' git me a woman, an' put aside the rest of that money fo' a rainy day, suh. Colonel, you been good to me an' I'll do anythin' in the worl' for you, but I got a hundred dollars, suh, an' I got to go wheah I'll be safe!"

"To North Carolina," said Blayde. "Yes."

He had a notebook. He wrote on a leaf and tore it out.

To Any Federal or Former Confederate Officer or Official:

The bearer of this note, named Jode, has been my servant. He has been faithful and honest, and the horse he rides was given to him by me. To my knowl-

edge he has broken no laws of the United States or
Confederate governments. I bespeak your kindness
to him.

BLAYDE HOLLISTER
Late Colonel, C.S.A.

He read it to Jode and handed it to him.

"That won't do you a bit of good with bushwhackers,"
he admitted, "and you'd better ride as much as you can
by night till you get across the Mississippi. But most white
men will think it means something, if you get into
trouble."

"All white men, suh," said Jode earnestly. "Thank you,
suh!"

He hesitated. Blayde shook hands with him. Jode wept
a little. Then he left. When Blayde, carrying his own
saddlebags, paid for his hotel accommodations and went
to the corral to saddle up, Jode was gone. He had evidently tested the note's efficacy right away. The corral proprietor had traded him a rusty pistol—still shootable, however—for the saddle the second horse had worn, and Jode
had gone off riding on a ragged saddle blanket and with a
rope bridle. A mile out of town he would pull off into the
woods and artfully go over the animal Blayde had given
him. When he was finished the mare would look unkempt
and ill fed and very probably afflicted with one or several
ailments that would make her undesirable even to a bushwhacker. By the time he reached the Mississippi, Jode
would have the smaller animal looking like a veritable
wreck of a horse. Nobody would want to steal her from
him. And he would be a pathetic figure until he got home.
Then he would blossom out as a rich man and tell his
descendants to the third and fourth generation about his
adventures with Colonel Reb Hollister when the Yankees
had regiments of soldiers hunting for him.

Blayde saddled up for a long day's ride. He went out
of town, looking over the lie of the ground in accordance
with Marshal Hickok's explicit directions. A little before
noon he had everything in mind and sat tranquilly in the

shade of an oak tree, watching for the St. Louis stage.

It was a particularly beautiful morning. Cattle driven to Springfield from Kansas and the southern plains were held in great herds on the farther side of the small log-and-plank town. Smaller bunches of cattle, bought by Eastern purchasers, moved on the trail to the East. Moving as they would move, through largely wooded country, they could not be handled in such numbers as the open plains permitted. Five hundred animals was a very large number of cattle to move in one herd across Missouri for the Atlantic seaboard. More often the trail bunches were three hundred or two hundred or even less, and it took many mounted men to watch and guard them.

There was one distant cloud of yellow dust where a herd that had started hours since was nearly to the point where low hills would hide it. There was a horse at the edge of town, methodically trying to buck its rider off, when it would—it did—turn and try to stamp him into mangled, bloody pulp. The rider hit the ground. A rope dragged the victorious horse, still fighting, away from its longed-for victim. There was a thin haze of dust rising above the false-fronted buildings on the town's main street. But the world, the great world of hills and trees and sun and sky, was utterly tranquil. Blayde could see for miles. The doings of men seemed particularly inane, in such peace and in such a setting.

There came a swiftly moving small-sized cloud of dust. Blayde could see the two leaders of the stage team clearly. He could see the next horses more or less in detail. The stage itself was a racketing, rolling, lightly built vehicle carrying six passengers inside. Nobody was insane enough to ride outside with the driver in the dust.

It looked like a very pretty toy, from the distance and height from which Blayde regarded it. It traveled briskly toward the town.

Blayde threw a leg over his horse. Perhaps it was the feeling that here on the frontier he had left behind the tragedy of a fallen Confederacy and the grim spitefulness of a beginning Reconstruction. Perhaps it was the highly original bargain he had made with Marshal Hickok. Possibly it was only the quiet and peace and brightness of the morning. In any case, he felt singularly cheerful. There was no great reason to be especially encouraged about his quest for the Marlow brothers, but he felt almost lighthearted as he rode down into Springfield, timing his arrival so he'd get there just after the stage.

He rode into Springfield to get killed by Marshal Wild Bill Hickok. It was all arranged.

Chapter Four

H E TIMED IT just right. The stage had stopped in front of the town corral, and its horses were in the act of being led away from it. The driver said acidly to a passenger:

"Ma'am, the stages for the south an' west go in half an hour. You can git some vittles if you like, or do anything you've a mind to. This stage stays right heah."

The horses vanished in the corral gateway. Blayde leaned against the corner of a feed store across the street from the hotel. The wise dark head of Yank, the big horse, was just behind him in the alley. There had been half a dozen passengers on the stage, and some of them gaped at the look of Springfield. To persons from more repressed areas it had a strange appearance. But a man who looked like a cowboy minus his horse moved as if sheepishly down the main street, and a man who looked like a traveling salesman supervised the unloading of three sample cases from the stage's boot. That left one passenger staring about him with a depressed and dogged air. He was dressed in the manner of the East.

Blayde had himself been in Springfield a good deal less than twenty-four hours, but its viewpoint was contagious. It was a crude town, Springfield. It was raw and uproarious and not at all refined. But it was very much alive. It had affected Blayde already. The flamboyance of Marshal Wild Bill Hickok was not now displeasing to him. The idea of a dramatic scene, practically a stage presentation, on the main street of the town was not one that would have occurred to anyone east of the Mississippi River. But Hickok's zest had been infectious, and there was some common sense in the performance he proposed, at that. So Blayde found himself looking upon the street as a stage for the lurid sequence in which he was to play one of the two star parts. He even found himself more than a little inclined to smile.

44

The Easterner asked a question of the stage driver.

"How'd I know?" snapped the driver. "I don't keep track of Marshal Hickok. Ask somebody else."

"But he was to meet me," protested the Easterner.

"Mebbe somebody killed him," the driver snapped again.

"But he's the town marshal."

"Is that a reason he cain't be a corpse?"

The driver marched along the street and into a saloon. The Easterner picked up his Gladstone bag. There were people on the street, but those nearby were plainly busy. Loafers were to be seen half a block away, sitting in the shade of a storm porch, but Blayde was the only conspicuously idle person within conversational distance. The Easterner crossed the street to him.

"Excuse me," said the Easterner, "but I'm looking for Mr. Hickok."

His pronunciation placed him. New England. But his intonation placed him further. Boston. And Blayde might have been curt with a nasal-voiced Yankee—he had taken too many of them prisoner during the war—but there were New England gentlemen. They were still Yankees, but not as bad as Yankees who were not gentlemen. Blayde said gravely, being careful not to smile:

"So am I, sir."

"Er—have you any idea where he may be found?"

"He is in the hotel," said Blayde as gravely as before. "He should come out any minute now. I told him I would be here."

"Ah, an appointment," said the Easterner. He put down his bag to get out a cigar.

"I told him I would kill him," said Blayde in stately fashion.

Despite himself, his tone was not quite serious. The Easterner hesitated, and smiled painfully, and said:

"I look green, eh? I am. I admit it. Of course you're joking, Mr.—er—er—"

"Colonel," said Blayde shortly. "Hollister. Colonel Hollister, sir. Confederate States Army."

The Easterner said as ruefully as before, "I should get proper clothes, perhaps. I've been told tall tales all the way from St. Louis. It seems to be the custom. Of course you're pulling my leg. Colonel Hollister's an outlaw. I've seen posters calling for his arrest. You wouldn't be walking the streets here, quite openly, if—"

Blayde looked at him coldly. This man didn't frighten easily, even when what he was told happened to be quite true. Then he raised his eyes.

"There is your friend Hickok now," he said briefly. "You had best move aside."

· Wild Bill Hickok came out of the hotel and stood before the door. He deliberately raised one hand and stroked his flowing mustaches. He looked up the street and down it, deliberately ignoring Blayde. There was sudden movement everywhere. Men were moving quickly for cover. It had been agreed that Hickok would spread the word that Colonel Reb Hollister was in town and that he expected to arrest him on sight. With a reputation as a defiant rebel, Blayde would not be expected to submit quietly. Citizens of Springfield recognized a situation when they saw Blayde on one side of the street and Wild Bill Hickok on the other. In seconds there was not a man in sight save for Blayde and the Easterner and Wild Bill Hickok. There was a man driving a hide wagon some distance off, but a voice called a warning to him. He stopped the wagon, jammed on the brakes, and ran to be out of the way of flying lead. Then there were only peepings.

The Easterner did not observe this. He picked up his bag and went across the street, kicking up puffs of yellowish dust as he walked. He reached in his pocket and pulled out a letter.

"Mr. Hickok?" he said. "I have a letter for you from—"

"Duck!" snapped the town marshal.

He reached out a huge hand. It swept the Easterner aside and sent him sprawling.

Blayde started across the street. He was vexed to find himself enjoying this. He called in a harsh voice:

"Marshal, I hear you're looking for me!"

The marshal boomed, "This town is closed to outlaws, Colonel! You must have known it! Either you put up your hands or draw your pistol—and make your choice quickly!"

Blayde, still moving forward, cried fiercely, "I'm drawing!"

Like magic, there was a huge Colt in Hickok's hand. It roared. There was another, answering roar not a fraction of a second later, and Wild Bill's hat leaped and fell to the ground. His Colt bellowed again.

Blayde stumbled, took a half step more, and crumpled to the ground. He got off a single wild shot as he toppled.

Then there was silence in the street. Town Marshal Hickok reholstered his pistol. Men came into view again up the street. The Easterner struggled to his feet, shockingly pale.

"He— It was true!" he panted.

Wild Bill looked annoyedly behind him. No one came. He fixed the Easterner with a glittering, baleful eye.

"You!" bellowed Hickok. "You were in it with him! You were to hold my attention while he shot me down! And him with his horse ready for a getaway! Go get that horse!"

The Easterner licked his lips. "My name is—"

"You're his partner!" roared Wild Bill. The Easterner was not a small man, but Wild Bill towered over him. He shook the man from the stage coach. "I'll give—you—one— second—" roared Hickok, "to get that horse and bring it here! Move!"

The Easterner got the horse. Then he drew a deep breath as if to protest with it.

Hickok snapped, "Take his heels! Turn him over! Heave him up! So!"

He had Blayde's shoulders. He swung Blayde's weight upward almost without the other man's help. Blayde's limp form hung over the saddle. The Easterner protested:

"But Mr. Hickok, I—"

"You're one of his gang!" bellowed Hickok, with blaz-

ing eyes. "I give you three seconds to get him outa sight!
Take him away! Bury him! Or—"

Again a huge Colt appeared miraculously in his hand.

The Easterner doggedly retrieved his Gladstone bag,
which in itself called for courage of a sort. He took the
horse's reins. Tight-lipped, he led big Yank down the
alley between the stable and a restaurant. Partway down
the alley he saw a somehow horrifying sight. Blayde, sag-
ging over his saddle and with his hands trailing down to
the dust, was dragging Wild Bill Hickok's hat. One of his
fingers had caught in the hole his bullet had made.

The Easterner stopped short. And Blayde whispered
ferociously: "Keep moving! I've got another pistol!"

But he did not stir otherwise until the incredulous,
white-faced stranger had turned behind the building so
that they were invisible from the street where the shooting
fray had taken place. Then he slid off of Yank and said
quietly:

"You involved yourself, sir, in a private arrangement
between Mr. Hickok and myself. Perhaps the matter can
be straightened out. But right now you will come with
me!"

And he walked behind the Easterner, grimly, until the
outskirts of the town were reached. Then he put the Gladstone bag on his saddle and they marched toward the
hills.

He was at once amused and very much annoyed. Hickok had outlined the whole affair. From Wild Bill's stand-
point it was very good business. He was about to leave
Springfield for a career in the theatre in the Eastern states.
He would portray a frontier town marshal in a play in-
volving rather preposterous to-do over a young actress
whose charming innocence on stage did not keep her
from swearing like a trooper off. There were to be fine,
mouth-filling lines that Wild Bill would bellow to the
wide-eyed admiration of audiences everywhere, and he
would shoot off an incredible number of blank cartridges
at each performance. He would bask in the admiration
and in the splendor of the character he portrayed, and

he would actually try to carry some of its more melo-
dramatic mannerisms into real life when the theatrical
season was over. With such a career before him, to kill
the notorious Colonel Reb Hollister as a last official act
was sound sense. It would mean money in the box office.

That was Hickok's view. And he doubtless found a
childlike pleasure in contriving the pseudo killing as an
advance theatrical performance. It would strike him as a
very good joke on the world.

To Blayde it was no less common sense. It looked as if
the Marlow brothers had heard of his hunt for them and
had sent somebody to kill him. That man was dead back
in Greenville now. But the Marlows would be uneasy
when they did not hear from him. They could send somebody else. They would be on guard. But if Colonel Reb
Hollister were reported dead, under circumstances dramatic enough to make the story spread, the Marlow
brothers would be relieved. They would not be so hard
to find.

And then, when they were disposed of, if the recalci-
trant Confederate colonel Reb Hollister were officially
dead—why, the civilian Blayde Hollister could set about
building a new life for himself somewhere, provided that
he found a life he would want to build. At the moment
he couldn't picture one.

He walked sourly beside the Easterner who had become involved in the play-acting Wild Bill had designed.
He was disturbed. If the Easterner talked in town, the
results would be serious—for the Easterner. Wild Bill, certainly, would not allow any man to say that as a duelist
he was a fake. He wasn't. He had killed more men than
he could quite count up, and he honestly did not want
to kill any more. But he would not let himself be laughed
at.

At long last Blayde stopped where he had cached his
saddlebags. He tethered Yank and gloomily made a small
fire.

His prisoner said doggedly, "Well? Did you bring me
out here to murder me?"

"Hardly," said Blayde. "I was thinking of cooking some bacon for the two of us. It's been a long time since breakfast. We have to think things out." He prepared to cook, and said politely, "Do you prefer your bacon fat or lean?"

The Easterner said indignantly, "Who are you, anyway?"

"The name is Hollister," said Blayde, "as I told you. And I am actually the man they call Colonel Reb Hollister. I assure you, though, that the distinction isn't of my choice. It was forced upon me."

"My name," said the Easterner sharply, "is Weatherby. Martin Weatherby. I happen to be a United States marshal."

He stopped at Blayde's expression. "What's the matter?"

"Hickok was expecting you," said Blayde wryly. "But I don't think he recognized you as the marshal he looked for."

It appeared that a strictly local town marshal had driven a Federal officer out of Springfield at pistol point, in the act of faking a shooting fray. It was not good.

"Be that as it may," said Weatherby doggedly, "I am a United States marshal. And this may not be my proper district, but—"

Blayde cooked bacon over the fire, thinking with wry amusement of the picture of Hickok making a butt of a United States marshal, when he was expecting to be impressively polite to him.

"But," Weatherby said firmly, "since I do have the authority and the duty, I'm going to have to take you into Springfield and turn you over to the proper authorities. And if that fight in the street was feigned, as it appears to have been, Hickok is not a proper authority and I'll have to take over from him."

Blayde sat back from the fire and looked at his prisoner in frank amazement. The Easterner actually meant it. He was frowning, as if disturbed by the complexity of the situation in which he found himself, but plainly he had no intention of overlooking anything. He meant to try to do what he believed his duty. And Blayde found that his attitude toward this United States marshal was that of someone listening to a small boy talk gravely of his intention to perform impossibilities.

"There are a few facts of life to be considered, Mr. Weatherby," he said gently. "Such as—how are you going to manage it?"

Weatherby matter-of-factly pulled out a wallet from his pocket. He offered Blayde a document. It was impressive. It was signed by no less a personage than the attorney general of the United States, and it appointed one Martin Weatherby a United States marshal with authority and jurisdiction as such in Dallas County, Texas. Weatherby seemed to consider that the document took care of everything. Blayde read it with outward respect and returned it.

"It is unanswerable," he said mildly. "But since this bacon is so nearly done, we had better have something to eat."

Weatherby put the paper away. He suddenly realized that Blayde was not impressed. He moved restlessly about the fire. Blade expertly removed the bacon and offered Weatherby a tin plate. The Easterner ate in silence. Blayde ate thoughtfully, but once or twice the corners of his mouth twitched. Weatherby suddenly did not seem to be quite sure whether Blayde was his prisoner or he Blayde's. Blayde let him wonder. Of course, Weatherby had submitted to the threat of Hickok's pistol, but under the circumstances that was sense. Blayde would have done the same. Later Weatherby had been marched out here by Blayde. But he was not cowed. Bewildered, perhaps. Hopelessly unfitted for the post to which he had been appointed. But he evidently expected to try to do his duty, learning as he went along how it should be done. Only he wouldn't live long enough to learn. Blayde felt almost protective toward him. He had been shot at often enough by Yankees not to feel contemptuous of them as a class, and he had shot at enough of them not to hate them just because they had won the war.

After a long time he said meditatively, "Mr. Weatherby, I am beginning to worry."

Then he heard a sound. He stood up quickly, went to Yank, and jerked his rifle from the saddle holster.

"What's the matter?"

"Nothing yet," Blayde told him, "but until I know who this is, duck!"

He moved quietly to a place that commanded all approaches to his campfire. He had chosen this spot because such a place was nearby.

He waited. It was very silent everywhere. The sky overhead was very blue, with white clouds here and there. The trees on the hill slopes were very green, and the sunlight was bright and all the world shimmered.

Hoofbeats sounded on rock, and ceased. They came again, nearer. Then Wild Bill Hickok rode into view. He grunted as he saw Blayde waiting with a ready rifle.

"Colonel Hollister, suh," said Wild Bill reproachfully, "is it a friendly act to shoot a hole in my hat and then steal it?"

Blayde grinned.

"A precious relic," he said. "I couldn't resist it. Was the fight convincing to the citizens of Springfield?"

"The town, suh," said Hickok, "is picturing me off somewhere filing another notch on my gun. Your pistol, suh. Somebody wanted to grab it for a souvenir, but I took it as loot. I return it." He sighed and dismounted. "Yes, Colonel, in town they swear you are dead as a doornail."

"My corpse," said Blayde, "offers profound thanks. Can I cook you something, Marshal?"

Hickok shook his head. He looked at Weatherby and observed, his voice booming:

"I had a man was supposed to come out and heave you on your horse, Colonel, and lead you out of sight. But he stopped to get a drink and showed up late. So I had to pick on the little man here." He regarded Weatherby benignly. "Sorry I had to tin-can you, suh, but I had to get Colonel Reb out of town before the local folks found out we were play-acting."

Weatherby said resentfully, "This is ridiculous! You, a peace officer, pretending to shoot while actually aiding an outlaw wanted by the United States government!"

Wild Bill stared at him.

"And who might you be, suh, to tell me what I'm to do and what I'm not to?"

Blayde said with fine formality, "This is United States Marshal Weatherby, Mr. Hickok. He is the one you were expecting." He added, "Not bad, for a Yankee."

Weatherby frowned at Hickok. His face expressed disapproval and indignation, and no fear at all. And Hickok was accustomed to see people afraid of him, but someone brave enough to disapprove of him was a novelty. He looked at Weatherby and said in honest incredulity:

"But it—but it just ain't possible, Colonel! Look at him!"

"He's a United States marshal all right," Blayde assured him. "He showed me his Federal appointment paper."

Wild Bill looked at Weatherby, fascinated.

"Would you shoot something, suh?" he asked. "Please, suh!"

"My pistol is in my bag," said Weatherby uncomfortably. He was not at ease. "It's with my badge. You see, out of my own territory—"

Hickok, his face a study in curiosity, offered one of his own weapons. As Weatherby held it uneasily in his hand, Hickok said to Blayde:

"By the way, Colonel, I made inquiries, but that Box O brand, suh, isn't known heah. Texas is a big state. I learn that you can find out at the statehouse, in Austin, where the brand is registered from. My informant, himself a Texan, added that if, while you are there, you will shoot the governor, suh, all Texas will arise and call you blessed."

"Thanks," said Blayde.

Weatherby looked at him rather helplessly.

"What shall I shoot at? But this is absurd!"

"It's the best sense I know," said Hickok. "Hit anything, suh. That tree yonder."

Weatherby raised the pistol. He held it at arm's length, in the posture prescribed by the Officers' Manual for U. S. Volunteers, Issue of 1863, a manual mistakenly perused by aspirant Yankee officers until their first actual battle, when they threw it away with curses. Blayde recognized the pose and shook his head. Hickok stared.

The pistol bellowed. A bit of bark leaped from a rotted limb, feet out from the trunk and ten feet high.

There was dead silence. Weatherby's face turned red.

"I am—rather out of practice," he said stiffly.

Wild Bill Hickok tugged at his flowing mustache.

"I'd say, friend marshal," he observed, "that you are right bad out of luck. I'll shake your hand now, suh. I won't have a chance later. You'll be the shortest-lived marshal that ever came down the pike."

Weatherby flushed again. But he said doggedly, "I tried to explain to you earlier today, Mr. Hickok. I have a letter for you from the attorney general." He produced it from an inner pocket. "It asks you to accompany me to Dallas County, in Texas, where—well—someone with your ability as a peace officer is sorely needed."

Hickok grinned. "I've got other plans, Mr. Weatherby. The Colonel heah, he sort of helped me rehearse for them this noontime."

"But this letter's from the attorney general!" insisted Weatherby. "It puts the matter to you as a patriotic duty!"

"I've got duty scars all over me now," said Wild Bill, "and some I got from acting smart. This time I show sense. From now on, anybody who sees me shooting off a pistol is going to pay to watch it, suh. I'm leaving with Mr. Newell on the evening stage."

He retrieved his pistol from Weatherby's hand—the Easterner had been using it to gesticulate with—and turned to Blayde.

"Colonel, suh, it's been an honor to know you. We—ah—actors"—and he grinned broadly— "may only meet in passing, but you did my friend a great service, and my friends' friends are mine. Thank you, suh!"

He mounted. He was an impressive figure on a horse. He looked benignly down upon Weatherby, but to Blayde it seemed that he looked very tired. It occurred to Blayde that a man with a reputation like Wild Bill's would not sleep well of nights. When all one's waking hours must be spent in constant alertness, when one never leaves an open door or window in his rear, when it has become impossible to let anyone stand behind one for any reason, a man cannot relax thoroughly even in his own bed. So Wild Bill Hickok was tired. It showed. He would be glad to get away from places where any braggart or any fool would feel that to be famous he had to kill Wild Bill. He needed sleep. Sound sleep.

"But—this outlaw?" demanded Weatherby. "He is a wanted man! He must be arrested! This is not my official district, but if you don't arrest him, I'll have to!"

He was in earnest. Blayde found that he liked this foolish Yankee who had done nothing whatever successfully, and was entirely unqualified to do anything, and who was infernally likely to get himself killed trying to do something.

"Mr. Weatherby, suh," said Wild Bill patiently, "you are a long way from Boston. We had a war in neighboring parts not long ago. War upsets things, suh. You'll find men in high office who are thieves and cutthroats, and you'll find others branded as outlaws who are only fighting for the justice that's been denied them. Colonel Hollister did a favor to a friend of mine last night. My friend was a Yankee like yourself, Mr. Weatherby. The Colonel heah saved his life. Out of kindness. The Colonel fought in the war. He knows it's over, but some others don't. It's my opinion, suh, that you'd better learn to know a good man when you see one. It's a lot more important than learning how he stands with the law. Even as a law officer, suh, I can tell you that is sound advice."

He waved his hand to Blayde. He wheeled his horse about and rode away. When he had gone, Blayde said politely:

"He leaves on the evening stage. So I shall keep you

here until the stage has gone. If you went into Springfield, you might be tempted to tell the truth about this morning's affair, and that would be calling Mr. Hickok a liar, because he's told it differently. For both your sakes I shall keep you a prisoner until the stage has left."

"And then—"

Blayde shrugged. "I'm off for Texas. What you say about me won't bother me. Especially since nobody will believe you. Nobody would believe Wild Bill would fake a pistol duel. Even I have some reputation—"

Weatherby insisted, "If I try to leave, you'll shoot me?"

"In the leg," admitted Blayde.

"But—dammit!" Weatherby sat suddenly down on a rock, and said determinedly, "I don't understand this. You're prepared to shoot me but not to kill me. You kidnap me, but you do not rob me. You have no respect for the law, but—"

"It's a lot different from Boston," agreed Blayde.

Weatherby looked at him very earnestly for what seemed minutes. Then he said doggedly:

"I thought I was a man of experience. All this I am unprepared to cope with. Do you know, Mr. Hollister, I begin to doubt my own competence as a United States marshal?"

"You're something new in the way of a carpetbagger," said Blayde. "Even to want to be competent is a novelty!"

Weatherby said angrily, "I'm no carpetbagger! Incompetent, perhaps, but I did not get my appointment to grow rich on bribes! I'm a member of a railroad family. My father—er—builds railroads. He is a financier. There is thought of extending a railroad through Dallas County. That was my original interest in the place."

Blayde offered him a cigar, with all due courtesy. Weatherby went on, at once irritated and resolute:

"Then there developed—well, personal reasons. And it appears that there is a group of brigands terrorizing the district to which I got myself appointed. A group of brothers. Murderous scoundrels. They have to be taken care of."

Blayde said mildly, "The name? Of the brothers? It wouldn't by any chance be Marlow, would it?"

"Marlow?" Weatherby looked astonished. "Why, yes! That's the name. A poetic family. Bryant Marlow, William Marlow, Longfellow—"

"No," said Blayde. "The third is Cullen. William, Cullen, and Bryant."

He had gone suddenly very pale. He had been amused today, and he had been concerned. Now he was white and desperately tense.

"And they are in Dallas County, Texas?" he asked steadily.

"Yes." Weatherby fumbled. "The letter from the attorney general mentions them. Here it is. You know them?"

"I've never met them," said Blayde in an extraordinarily quiet fashion. "I've been looking for them for a long time, though."

He rose and went to his saddlebags. He came out with a thick, wrapped packet. He handed Weatherby a handbill, one of the posters he had put up all over Alabama and Missouri. It was the one offering five thousand dollars' reward, in Yankee greenbacks, for information leading him to the present hiding place of the Marlows. Weatherby read it through and stared hard at Blayde.

"But—these are the same men?"

"Yes," said Blayde briefly. "Hold out your hand, please. One hundred, two, three, four, five—"

"What on earth?" demanded Weatherby helplessly as greenbacks piled up in his palm. "What—"

"You've made yourself five thousand dollars," said Blayde with grim satisfaction. "And you may find your troubles simplified when you get to Dallas, Mr. Weatherby. I'm headed there now."

Then he stopped.

"It occurs to me," he said with an odd smile, "that the United States government is at odds with me just now. In fact, I'm an outlaw because the United States did not make peace with me when the war ended. But I am not

unfriendly on that account. You wanted Mr. Hickok to
go down with you to attend to the Marlows. I'd be glad
to take care of them for the government, which should
have attended to them in the first place."

Weatherby looked helpless. His hands were full of
money, and he was very dusty and horribly embarrassed
on a frontier hillside. Blayde regarded him estimatingly.

"I—I can't take this money!" said Weatherby. "It's impossible! It's—"

He did not quite say "stolen," but Blayde supplied the
term.

"Stolen? Oh, no. Even the Federal government doesn't
charge me with theft. I took that money in what is officially called a guerrilla raid—a military action, Mr.
Weatherby. I can be hanged for it, but it is not stolen.
And I promised to pay it for the news you just gave me."

"I can—return it to the government," said Weatherby
uneasily.

Blayde shrugged. "That's not my affair. The Marlows
are. I made you an offer you do not care for. But if you
are really going down to Dallas, sir, out of gratitude I
suggest that you ride with me. I might—" his tone was
very dry—"be of some use on the way. Frankly, I think
you need a few lessons. Not about the bees and the flowers,
but on how to use a pistol, and matters of that sort."

Weatherby frowned. The sheaf of greenbacks in his
hand bewildered him. But suddenly he put them in his
pocket.

"I don't know you, Mr. Hollister," he said painfully,
"and in Boston this would be most irregular. You're
branded as an outlaw, a Southern guerrilla. But in a peculiar way I have to believe that you are also an honest
man. I begin to see that there may be something in what
Hickok said. And you are more capable than I am. If
you will allow me, I will travel with you. After all, my
purpose in going to Dallas would not be served by getting
myself killed out of hand. Even my—ah—personal object
would not be gained by that. And I—I really would like
to accept your offer to be my deputy, Mr. Hollister. After

all, I did mean for Mr. Hickok to go with me. You could
take his place, and I am sure you would be most efficient.
But—after all, to have a known outlaw for a deputy . . ."

"The outlaw was killed this noontime," Blayde re-
minded him. He grinned. His ways of thinking were
changing remarkably. Since the day before, he had realized that life in the West was only secondarily a pattern
of action. First it was a state of mind, which was a con-
genial one. "And also, Mr. Weatherby, I wouldn't think
of being your deputy. I suggest that you think about being
mine."

"Yours?" Weatherby was bewildered again. "I don't
see . . ."

"Colonel Reb Hollister is dead," repeated Blayde, sav-
oring the flavor of his words as he spoke them. "But I
could be United States Marshal—Weatherby is the name?
Yes. In that capacity I think I could handle the situation.
And as *my* deputy, you would be in a position to see to
it that I did."

He flung his saddlebags over Yank's back and deftly
strapped them in place.

"Think it over," he advised briefly. "Right now we'd
better head for a chuck wagon somewhere near one of
those herds of waiting cattle. It wouldn't do for me to go
into town—I'm dead—and you'll need to buy a saddle and
a horse."

Yank, by now, followed Blayde about like a dog. Blayde
made a gesture and started off on foot. Weatherby came
after him, wearing a peculiar expression on his face.

Chapter Five

T HE WORLD moved on. Events of earth-shaking impor-
tance took place here and there. The provisional government of Spain scornfully posted Queen Isabella's procla-
mation, outlawing all its members, in prominent places
in Madrid. Admiral Henry H. Bell, of the Asiatic Squad-
ron, U. S. Navy, was drowned when his barge was
swamped on a bar in the harbor of Hyogo, Japan. Twelve
seamen perished with him. He was given an impressive
funeral. There was an earthquake and tidal wave at
Arica, in Peru. Events of enormous and permanent sig-
nificance took place and were duly chronicled in the
newspapers.

But it went unreported that there was a canopy of
stars above the prairie. On a certain night there was a
campfire burning. There were two horses tethered nearby.
And Blayde Hollister said matter-of-factly:

"Yes, you're doing better. A great deal better. But a
heavy-caliber bullet tears a prairie chicken to pieces when
it hits the body. You will want to be able to knock their
heads off when you shoot them. That will come in time."

"I aimed at the head of this one," admitted Weatherby
forlornly. "I'm not a good shot."

"Not yet," admitted Blayde. "You haven't been shooting all your life."

They were well on the way down toward Texas. Blayde
was nursing Weatherby along. At first he'd felt a sort of
scornful tolerance for the Easterner, motivated by a com-
bination of relief that through him a clear trail now ex-
isted to the Marlows and a sort of pity for anybody so
unfitted for life beyond the confines of civilization.

Weatherby was inept. He had only resolution to qualify
him for the outskirts of the modern world. For one thing,
he simply did not think, as was necessary, in terms of
possible hostility directed against himself. He had never

been robbed, never insulted, he had never even been the victim of a pickpocket. Even his riding was distinctively that of someone who had known none but well-trained horses of proven spirit but equally well-demonstrated docility.

Slowly, now, he was acquiring something like a veneer of the habits needed to survive beyond the farthest reach of the newest railroad. He could, now, cook beans. He could fry bacon. He had learned to clean a wild turkey, and his way with coffee was becoming tolerable, though he still hadn't gotten used to the sort of beverage considered drinkable on the plains. Blayde took to that at once. Having drunk all during the war a coffee made from roasted acorns and dandelion roots, Blayde reveled in the beverage native to the West. Beyond the Mississippi, coffee that was doubtfully strong could be tested—so the tale was—by putting a wedge of iron in it. If the wedge sank, the coffee was too weak. Weatherby's coffee was often doubtful; Blayde's never.

But Weatherby's shooting appeared to be hopeless. With a rifle he was bad, but not unthinkably so. With a pistol in his hand, however, he was completely harmless to man or beast. Blayde tried with infinite pains to rectify the situation. It could not be done. Still, having dubiously accepted the company of an outlawed man, Weatherby behaved with proper humility, and at least he never complained. As a Bostonian and a law-abiding man, he disapproved of Blayde, but he had come to practice a hesitant friendliness in which the hesitation plainly came from moral considerations alone.

They smoked beside the fire. Presently they would put it out and move well away from it before going to sleep. They would move their horses, also. Blayde had patiently explained the reason. There were no police on the plains. There were honest men there, but also there were scoundrels. Unless one of the two travelers stayed awake on guard, should they camp by a fire they might awake to find themselves looking into gun muzzles in the hands of completely conscienceless thieves, or even more likely they might not awake at all. They had found one skeleton by a campfire's ashes. There was absolutely nothing to tell who the man had been or where he was going. There was only a bullet hole in his skull to tell how he had died. And absolutely nothing, not even a cooking pot, had been left behind by whoever had killed him.

An eerie sound came through the night. Weatherby started and looked at Blayde.

"Coyote," said Blayde. "I heard them in Missouri. There are more of them here."

This was Oklahoma. Missouri was the West. Kansas City was the Far West. Beyond the plains were fabled Colorado and the Dakotas and the other territories. Somewhere there was Utah—Deseret. California was a name. There were emigrant routes by which covered-wagon trains sometimes made the journey, but the sensible route to California was still around the Horn by sailing ship. A more reckless but still preferable way was through Panama. But Missouri was West, and parts of Louisiana were West, and all of Texas. Beyond Texas there were other vague names—Arizona Territory and the like—which were synonyms for desert and thirst and Indian fighting.

The fire crackled softly and gave off a smoke and an odor that itself was unfamiliar. Blayde was quietly satisfied. He fitted in here. But the face of the Easterner was troubled.

"Do you think I shall ever be able to hold up my end out here?" he asked unhappily.

"In time," said Blayde. He cocked his ears. Yank snorted, off in the darkness. But it was only some minor irritation. Buffalo flies, at a guess.

"I'm not so sure," said Weatherby ruefully. "It seemed so simple, back in Boston. There was trouble in Dallas County. My father is interested in plans for a railroad. I became interested, too, and of course . . ."

Blayde said nothing. He looked at his cigar. When it was finished, they would extinguish the fire and move on to bed down for the night. He was on his way to find the

Marlow brothers. It was good to be in motion toward a known achievement. He had felt this way during the war sometimes, when he knew where he was leading his regiment and for what purpose.

"I met Antonia," said Weatherby. He added hesitantly, "Do you mind if I talk?"

Blayde shook his head.

"I met her," said Weatherby slowly, "and it struck me—it still strikes me—as extraordinary. It's always astonishing, I suppose, to meet a woman who is different from every other woman, no matter where or when. But the odds against my meeting Antonia were enormous. She was in Boston. The odds against her being in Boston were incalculable. The odds against my meeting her were even greater. You see, my family is—conservative."

He looked at Blayde. Red, flickering firelight smote on both their faces. They were more suitably attired for the plains than they had been. Buckskin jackets had taken the place of broadcloth. Wider-brimmed hats had proved their utility. Even Weatherby wore completely practical boots now, instead of citified shoes, and he carried a pistol in his belt. It did not hang right and never would, but he was nearly used to it.

"I don't know whether you know how conservative a family can be," he added awkwardly.

"I do," said Blayde dryly.

He did. When he went away to war, his father had been concerned about his safety, to be sure, but almost as much disturbed about the sort of associates he might be thrown with. Only his mother had been sure he would not be contaminated. And his sister. Blayde put the thought away. He was on the trail of the Marlows now.

Weatherby said raptly, "I met Antonia at a dinner in Beacon Street. She was visiting one of the Farquehars. She had attended a female seminary with Martha Farquehar," added Weatherby conscientiously, "and the Farquehars are—their social position is such that whatever they do automatically becomes conservative and proper. But Antonia's family background was sound. Not Bostonian, of course. But her family is very old, even by Bostonian standards. The Robles' gave a viceroy to New Granada, and the senior branch of the family— But you would not be interested. Martha Farquehar told me the genealogy. One of them helped to pull down the Spanish flag when Mexico became free. One of Antonia's uncles was killed at the Alamo. Her father helped run up the American flag when Texas joined the Union."

Blayde said dryly, "Did none of them help haul it down for the Stars and Bars?"

"Y-yes," admitted Weatherby unhappily. "They did."

Blayde smiled at him. "Then I will concede that the family is respectable."

"You will remember that I fought at Chickamauga," said Weatherby quietly, "and I had a brother at Gettysburg. He—stayed there. We were private soldiers, not officers. We thought it—required of us."

Blayde's expression changed. He said gently, "My friend, I joked."

"Yes," said Weatherby. He made a little gesture with his hands. "I met Antonia. And I—simply looked at her, and —I wasn't a Bostonian or a Weatherby any longer. Such a thing had never happened to me before. I did not know it could happen. I had thought that one chose a wife with discretion, with thought, with proper consideration of practical affairs. Family and so on. But I simply looked at her, and I knew that all my family training meant nothing at all. I would have asked her to marry me had she been—anybody or anything. All this happened before I had so much as spoken to her. When Martha Farquehar introduced us, it was as much as I could do to keep from saying that I loved her then. You see—I did love her."

Blayde regarded him very curiously in the firelight.

"She told me afterward that she knew it when I took her hand. She was astonished that such a thing could happen in Boston. She said that it—pleased her. Did anything like that ever happen to you?"

Blayde shook his head. He had gone to war when he was still too young to have a sweetheart. He had been

married to his regiment during the war. And afterward
there was the matter that filled his time now. He suddenly noticed that Weatherby was no older than himself. It
had not occurred to him before, because Weatherby's
patient conscientiousness had somehow seemed elderly.
But now he realized that Weatherby was certainly not
over twenty-three. He had simply been raised so that he
was helpless away from the things he knew. Even in the
war, most likely, he had been in a company suitably
raised among the best families of Boston, with private
soldiers as aristocratic as the officers.

"I am completely ignorant of romantic matters," said
Blayde. "I have been—too busy."

Weatherby nodded.

"It was—very wonderful," he said, groping for words.
"Of course, I was glad that her family and background
were such that my family could approve. It meant that I
did not have to defy them. Martha Farquehar explained
it to them. Martha was a very good friend to Antonia and
to me. She is a wonderful girl. I have known her all my
life. I—really thought that someday we would marry. But
when I saw Antonia I knew. That very instant. Martha
cried when I told her—for joy, she said, that Antonia had
accepted my addresses."

Blayde watched him with genuine curiosity. One does
not fight through a war and end up leading a regiment
while remaining completely ignorant of human actions
outside of the battlefield. But Weatherby was something
new in Blayde's experience. Actually, the romance he
spoke of must have been the most commonplace of affairs.
A well-brought-up girl met a well-brought-up young man
at a party of well-brought-up people. They fell in love,
there were no obstacles not of their own contriving, and
it was altogether like thousands or millions of other ro-
mances. But Weatherby was transfigured, even only telling about it. As he sat awkwardly by a campfire under
a canopy of stars, with a pistol hanging uneasily at his
hip, his face seemed to shine a little.

"She got her family's permission, by mail, to become

engaged to me," he said in a hushed voice. "We were very happy. She went home by steamer to Galveston. Her father and brother met her there and she wrote me from their ranch, the Hacienda del Norte. It was understood that I was to come down and meet her family. Then it developed that there were local troubles. This group of outlaws, the Marlows, were creating a great deal of difficulty. I understand that they steal cattle and rob, and even the highways are unsafe. And my father is interested in a projected railroad that will pass through Dallas County. For the furtherance of the plans of the railroad, lawlessness should be put down. He exerted his influence and had me appointed a United States marshal for the district. He arranged for Marshal Hickok to be asked to go with me. It seemed a very practical, reasoned arrangement."

Blayde nodded. It was a very sensible arrangement for an influential Boston family to secure a Federal appointment for its son, and then to arrange for a thoroughly qualified gun fighter to be his deputy and take all the risks and do the work—for adequate pay, of course.

It should have been an eminently conservative and intelligent move. But Wild Bill Hickok had plans of his own, and this Weatherby was just a little better man than the son of such a Boston family should be. Without a seasoned fighting man beside him, he was doggedly going to try to carry out his plan alone. And he wouldn't live through it. He'd be killed.

"She is the most beautiful girl," said Weatherby, very simply, "that God ever made. When she walks across a room, somehow it is the most graceful movement that could possibly be imagined. When she smiles—" He fumbled for words. "I read a great deal of poetry when I was in college. I thought I knew something about romance and beauty and such things. 'But poetry is nonsense. It tries to say things there are no words for. I don't believe poets know, anyhow. . . . When Antonia smiles it's warm and friendly and sweet, but it's the fact that it is Antonia smiling that makes it so. Nobody else could

possibly smile like that. You can't say that in poetry—
or anyhow. Her voice isn't like bells or flutes or any
poetic simile anybody could ever think of. It's—" He
stopped, helplessly. "You hear it and you don't think of
bells or flutes. You think of Antonia, and you're glad.
There isn't anything you can liken her to. But if you
hear of something that's interesting or pleasant, you think
instantly that Antonia will enjoy hearing of it. When you
see something beautiful—like sunset today—you wish instantly that she were with you to look at it too. Even—"
He looked puzzledly at Blayde. "You know, I rather like
you, Blayde. I realized it when I thought I'd like Antonia
to know you. Of course, you're an outlaw—"

Then Blayde grinned at him. He tossed his cigar into
the campfire and rose. He kicked dirt over the coals.

"My respectable friend," he said, "you honor me. But
I have to acquire even a name before I can be presented
to her. Colonel Reb Hollister is dead. Wild Bill Hickok
killed him."

He pulled up the picket pins. Weatherby followed him
dutifully as they moved away into the dark, each of them
leading a horse.

"We come to a settlement tomorrow," added Blayde.
"We should lay in some supplies."

Weatherby trudged after him, lost in thoughts of the
girl he'd talked about tonight for the first time.

"Someday," said Blayde, moving ahead through black-
ness, "I'd like to borrow something from you, Martin.
Having no identity of my own, I'd like to borrow yours.
It would be interesting to feel like Martin Weatherby."

Weatherby said, "Certainly," in an absent voice. He
was still thinking of his Antonia.

They went on for nearly a mile, the two animals plod-
ding patiently behind them. If anybody had seen their
campfire and waited for it to die down, they might have
been seen to leave it, but they could hardly be followed
quietly in such darkness.

Again they picketed the horses. They rolled themselves up in their blankets—Weatherby had grown accus-

tomed to taking off his clothes only when there was an
opportunity to wash—and lay quiet. Blayde stared up at
the stars, thinking with an odd intentness of Weatherby.
He had a singular sense of responsibility for the other
man. Weatherby seemed so much younger now, somehow, because it was more clear how sheltered his whole
life had been.

I'd like to have seen the infantry company he was in,
thought Blayde with some grimness. His own regiment—

He suddenly yearned over those men who had followed
him. He felt a sickening homesickness for the compan-
ionship of men who had believed in him, and who had
not noticed his youth—he had not been conscious of it
himself—because they trusted him. He felt an aching
loneliness when he thought that the regiment had ceased
to be with the Confederacy. And there was nothing left
to take its place. There was a heap of weathered ashes
where he had been born, and graves held the only three
people who had ever loved him. All he had left was an
obligation to kill the Marlows. That was his only actual
possession. Even Weatherby, inept and unskilled as he
was, had infinitely more. He had a girl whose smile was
warm and friendly and sweet, whose voice was soft and
clear, and all herself; and who was the sort of person
who made you think, when you heard of something
pleasant or interesting, that she would be glad to hear
it, and whom you wished for whenever you saw anything
that was beautiful or anyone you respected or admired,
because you would like to share that with her too.

Blayde thought vaguely that he would like to believe
in a girl like that. He looked up at the stars, meditating
on what it must be like to feel like Weatherby, until
sleep came.

When morning arrived they rode on. For some reason
neither of them had much to say. Weatherby may have
been embarrassed because he had talked so much about
himself the night before. He had asked Blayde once,
bluntly, why he was an outlaw. Blayde had told him dis-
passionately, including the action of a Yankee captain in

Valdosta who had tried to arrest him when he asked for news of the murderers of his family. But Blayde had told it briefly and without emphasis. Last night, Weatherby had talked at length.

It was an unusually windy morning. There were thin clouds overhead, and the sunlight that did strike through was hardly warm. Dried grass blades and thistledown and dust went rushing over the gently rolling ground. Sometimes small dust whirls raced about erratically. The two horses and the two men plodded on.

They were three hours from their sleeping place when specks appeared far away. Two specks. They were mounted men, riding hard downwind. There was no destination behind Blayde and Weatherby for men to be hastening to.

Dust arose and hid the other riders. It swirled away, and they were nearer. They seemed to change their direction a little, to come closer to the line that Blayde and Weatherby followed.

Weatherby looked, and said nothing. As the figures drew closer, though, Blayde unconsciously loosened his pistols in their holsters.

"Why did you do that, Blayde?" asked Weatherby. He saw no reason for the precaution.

Blayde shrugged. "No reason," he admitted. "Just that they aren't going anyplace in such a fashion. There's noplace to go. So they must be coming from someplace. And they're in an almighty hurry. Coming straight for us, too."

Weatherby watched earnestly. There was a piebald horse and a roan. There was a big man and a smaller one. They were riding hard, over an empty plain with hurrying masses of dust and dried grass running foolishly about underfoot.

"They're spurring," added Blayde, after a moment.

Wind buffeted him. He and Weatherby went on, watching the approaching horsemen. One of the two men was hatless.

They came on at full speed and reined in furiously

almost on top of the two travelers. The big man panted:

"We're takin' yore hawsses! Don't start nothin'!"

Each of the newcomers had a pistol in his hand. The little man was bleeding from a nick along his jawbone. The big man panted, his face working. He was barely six feet from Blayde, and his desperation was evident. Blayde looked at him with the cynical alertness one learns in war.

"Git off!" panted the big man. "Both of you."

Weatherby's face turned obstinate. The smaller man seemed to gasp for breath, but his pistol pointed waveringly at Weatherby from nearly as short a distance. He made motions with the hand holding the weapon. The motions were commands to dismount. But Weatherby's expression was not that of one who planned to obey. Blayde knew, irritably, that he was getting set to fight. He said:

"Hold your horses, fellas. I'm getting off."

He put his hands on his saddle horn and swung to the ground. It looked like prompt surrender. But in order to move away from his horse he had to move his hands. He had to have them momentarily out of sight of the big man. A soldier would have realized that. The big man did not.

Blayde fired under Yank's neck. Twice. The first bullet crashed into the pistol menacing Weatherby. The second seemed to explode in the big man's hand. The weapon in that hand flew upward, disintegrating as it flew, and the big man groaned and clutched at his wrist.

"Don't try to draw that other pistol!" warned Blayde.

Weatherby had his pistol out now. He swallowed, and abruptly seemed to rage.

"Look heah!" panted the big man desperately. "I'm —we got to keep goin'! We need yore hawsses! I'm—I'm the town marshal of Callao, back yonder. I got to get help!"

The little man swore despairingly, nursing a numbed hand. He stared behind him apprehensively.

"I got to get help!" repeated the big man desperately.

"I'm the town marshal! There's a gang of Texas men in that town, an' they' hurrahin' it to a fare-you-well! They swore they was goin' to lynch us! I'm the town marshal! See my badge? I got to get help!"

Weatherby said in a flat voice, not at all consistent with the look of pure fury on his face, "I don't believe it."

Blayde moved with professional caution. There was a second pistol at the big man's hip. He took it. He moved to the smaller man. He'd carried only one weapon, and that was gone. The horses of the two fugitives were nearly blown. Blayde looked at the horizon. It was empty.

"Cover them," he said shortly to Weatherby. "We'll look into this little affair."

The big man panted and reiterated his frantic assertion that he had to go on and that he was the town marshal of Callao. He shook in his saddle. Blayde said no word to him. The smaller man merely swore helplessly. Blayde briskly and efficiently roped their feet under their horses' bellies. He knotted their bridles to a lead rope. He remounted.

"We'll go now."

He moved on, towing his captives behind him. He had spoken only three times since the affair began. The big man bellowed frantic pleas from the end of the rope. Weatherby reined in closer, his eyes still hot and angry.

"I was no good then," he said furiously. "I was just going to try to shoot him when you fired. Why did you have to shoot at my man first?"

"He only had to pull the trigger," said Blayde reasonably, "and if he jumped when I shot, you'd have been killed. The other man had to change his aim *and* fire. It was only common sense."

The big man bellowed again. Weatherby said:

"What do you think this means, anyhow?"

"We'll find out," said Blayde. He looked sidewise at Weatherby. "If he is the town marshal, and I've messed him up, I'll be in a better state to argue if I'm a United States marshal."

Weatherby fumed. Then he reached in his pocket and
brought out a small jeweler's box. He handed the pin
in it to Blayde. It was a gold badge. It was undoubtedly
the gift of a very proud family to Weatherby.

"Go on and wear it," said Weatherby bitterly. "I'm no
good!" Then he repeated, "But what does it mean—
what he says?"

Blayde continued to ignore the hoarse, frenzied bellowings to his rear. The two prisoners back there tried desperately to turn their horses aside. Without reins, they
failed. With only one functioning hand apiece, they
could not free their feet from the rope Blayde had tied.
They had to follow.

"I've had my men try to act like this," said Blayde
matter-of-factly. "Sometimes men have to let off steam.
It looks like a trail herd came by Callao and the trail
hands rode into town and they started kicking up their
heels. Our friends tried to stop them and didn't know
how. They were run up a tree. They've got the whole
town treed, if he's telling the truth."

The peculiar cavalcade topped a gentle rise. A long
way away there was a tiny town in sight. Off to one side
a slow-moving river of horned animals moved with a
monstrous deliberation. A rider went from the herd into
the town. A rider went back from the town toward the
herd. Blayde considered. The bellowings from behind
him grew shrill with anguished terror. He ignored them.

"Stay here, Martin," he commanded. "I'll go in, as a
United States marshal. Drag our friends up close, so the
three of you will look like a posse waiting for orders.
Don't let that piebald horse show. They might recognize it."

The wind still blew and dust still swirled, but faint
poppings came from the town. Blayde put Yank to a
brisk trot and rode in.

As he entered the main and only street, he saw a dead
man lying in the highway. Instantly the whole affair
changed complexion. To hurrah a town was an admissi-
ble if alarming diversion. It consisted of turning the town

painstakingly upside down, shooting out lights and windows, chasing citizens on the streets with bullets fired
about their feet, and the treating of all law and order
with contumely. But it did not involve killings unless
by accident, and since killings were not a part of the festivity, a killing should stop the festivity at once. Here,
it had not.

A woman screamed in stark, agonized terror. There
was no one in the street. There was tumult and uproar
in at least one of two saloons, but this scream came from
a sod house at the edge of town.

Blayde was off his horse and running in before the
scream ended. Inside the house a woman struggled with
a man in range costume. A citizen lay on the floor.

Without a word, Blayde fired.

He went out of the house and to the next one. The
door was battered in. The house was empty. He went
on to the next. Yank ambled patiently after him, like a
dog.

At the third house the door was open. A fat woman
with gray hair, sweat streaming down her face, danced
hysterically while a bearded man held a pistol to a fat
man's head and howled with amusement. As Blayde
entered he was saying, obviously not for the first time:

"When you stop dancin' he goes to glory."

Blayde, in the doorway, said, "No."

The man with the pistol turned blankly. He jerked
his weapon around to bear on Blayde. It did not yet
bear on him when Blayde's pistol spouted smoke and
flame.

Blayde reloaded painstakingly. This was not a hurrah.
This was a raid, a raid such as Quantrell's guerrillas had
carried out more than once during the war. It did not
take many men to make such a raid. Men with arms in
their hands and a concerted purpose have an enormous
advantage over civilians. A cold-blooded murder or two
establishes a sort of momentum of ascendancy. A dozen
men, acting together and on their own timetable and
with their own purposes, can overawe and loot a town

of a thousand people, provided only that they move fast and keep moving. Here was a mere hamlet. As many men as seemed to be here could disarm it and rule it indefinitely, until somebody came in with a greater ruthlessness than theirs.

Blayde was able to calculate the time this raid had been in progress by the distance the town marshal had been able to flee. He had run his horse out in panic-stricken flight of less than half an hour. The center of festivity was still the town's saloons. Shots came from one of them, with the sound of smashing bottles.

Blayde went in the door. There were seven men standing against the wall with their hands held high. Three others amused themselves hilariously. One man lay on the floor with an ominous pool of dark red flowing from his body.

Blayde was pale. His eyes burned with the blood lust he felt at memory of the Marlow brothers. One of the three armed men inside held a gun on the bartender, commanding drinks, while the others shot bottles from the bartender's hands as he shakily tried to obey. They were already nearly drunk. One of them missed the bottle of the moment, and the bartender's arm crimsoned.

Blayde opened fire without a challenge and without mercy. One of the three got in two shots before he crumpled to the floor.

"How many are there?" Blayde asked then, in a cold passion, thinking of Quantrell's men and the Marlows. "You men get their pistols and follow me!"

He went out. Men came surging after him, swearing in thick, deadly voices. The initiative had passed from the raiders to the citizens with the coming of Blayde. The mere fact that he was a newcomer, arriving after all the town was cowed, gave him an advantage out of all reason. He had actually shot down five men, simply because the raiders considered that nobody remained in the town with the will to fight.

They learned otherwise when Blayde led a clean-up.

One man in the other saloon. A man coming out of the general store. There was another man in that building. He holed up behind flour barrels until the citizens blasted him out, shooting with maniacal hate. Even so, he wounded two men before he died with a dozen bullets in him.

"Now get horses," said Blayde grimly. "Their horses. We're going out to the herd."

He had given all the orders. Nobody questioned his authority. Some had seen him kill three raiders. Perhaps others knew of his interference with those of the raiders who had been amusing themselves elsewhere than in the saloon. Possibly someone noticed the golden badge on his shirt. In any case, he had the habit of command and he was white with a terrible fury, and nobody thought of disobeying him.

There were five men with the herd. Only two of them were armed. They saw the raging, deadly group come from the town. One tried shooting. The other fled. A youngish man from the settlement dismounted and aimed a rifle with infinite care. The report came. The fleeing rider fell out of the saddle, with his foot caught in his stirrup. His horse stopped, trembling, a good half mile farther on.

The three unarmed men rode to the group, their hands held high. Raging and bitter, they said that this was a herd from the KY and Box Star X and several smaller ranches, headed up to Kansas City or Springfield from northern Texas. Some extra hands had been taken on for the trail, the owning ranches being shorthanded. Three days ago there had been shooting in the night. Men on night herd were killed in cold blood by those who went to relieve them. Men in their blankets by the chuck wagon were shot dead as they slept. New men arrived, by arrangement with the most recently hired hands. They left three of the original crew alive, disarmed, to do all the work of the camp and the herding. They were to be killed before the cattle reached the place where they were to be sold. It was one of the largest rustling operations undertaken to date. It would have meant the theft of a trail herd of over two thousand animals.

And it would have been successful but for the fact that, passing near the hamlet of Callao, the rustler-bandits could not resist the opportunity for a little fun. Perhaps they had intended merely to hurrah the town in traditional fashion. But they had let themselves get out of hand. There were three men and a woman killed in the town. There had been eleven rustlers. There weren't any, now.

Blayde calmed slowly, when it was all over. When he rode on with Weatherby, he was grimly silent for a long time. Then, with the town a mere spot upon the horizon behind them, he managed to smile.

"Lucky you lent me your badge," he said. "I hadn't any right to act like I did, tying up their marshal and all. But they didn't fuss about it when I said I was United States Marshal Weatherby."

Chapter Six

O NCE upon a time, when Texas was a part of Mexico, there was a Scotchman. He was surrounded by men of Spanish descent, and part-Spanish descent, and part-part-Spanish descent. They were ignorant and proud, and he robbed them enjoyably by close trading that they were at once too prideful and incompetent to imitate. His name is unknown. It was unpronounceable to those accustomed to Spanish. Only his business acumen is recorded, and the fact that in his cups—drinking tequila and aguardiente and even more heady beverages in default of Scotch whisky—he was wont to sing a wistful song in a roaring bass voice and a thick Scotch accent. The part his hearers remembered was a single line: "Green grow the rushes, oh . . ."

He was often in his cups. He often sang the song—and his name was unpronounceable to lips accustomed to Spanish. His bemused customers spoke of him as "Green g'o," from what they could recall of his song. In Spanish orthography that is "Gringo." It is an otherwise unknown Scotchman's immortality on earth. He provided the local name for the men who scorned, cheated, and ultimately took Texas away from its native inhabitants.

Blayde Hollister and Martin Weatherby arrived at a place where they were gringos. They arrived, in fact, in Dallas County, then newly formed from the western part of Nacogdoches and the eastern part of Robertson Counties. The law-enforcement officers of both parent counties were much relieved. The county was large and black-soiled. It contained the town of Dallas and the Trinity River, which—civilization had progressed so far—was already crossed by three bridges and a ferry for effeminate persons who did not like to swim their horses.

During the war it had sent many of its men into the Confederate Army. It did not get nearly so many of them

77

back. It had been the residence of Doc Holliday—originally from Valdosta, Georgia, by the way—who was a practicing dentist there until his paroxysms of coughing drove his patients away. He turned gambler, inevitably became a gun fighter, though he also used a knife on occasion, and killed at least eighteen other men during his career—the first one in Dallas. The town had also been visited by John Younger, who made a bet that he could shoot a pipe out of a smoker's mouth, was slightly drunk at the time, and shot off the tip of the smoker's nose instead. He then killed Sheriff Nichols when the sheriff moved to arrest him.

But there were oases of tranquillity and of even stately living within the limits of Dallas County. There was, for example, the sprawling Hacienda del Norte, whose herds had been uncountable. Even now, no two countings gave concordant results. Its rambling adobe dwelling had been built when fortification was needed against Indians, in the days when a viceroy from Madrid held court in Mexico City.

Those fortifications still guarded it, though not against Indians. The Indians had left, crowded out by less peaceful white men and Mexican immigrants. The sentries now carried rifles instead of harquebuses, and they watched against rustlers and bandits instead of feather-ornamented red men. But still they were needed.

Inside the hacienda, though, the traditional tempo of life and its graciousness remained. In the deeply shadowed, high-ceilinged rooms, Antonia Robles lived and moved and had her being. She had been born there and raised there. Now she waited for the well-brought-up young man to whom she had been affianced to come there and meet her family with due formality. Her father fought savagely to keep his herds from rustlers who throve unreasonably. At home he was a gentle, quiet man of culture. Her brother, Luis, tried angrily to use a leg that a Minie ball had stiffened, and to reconcile himself to the fact that the cause he had fought for was lost. He ended by hating all *yanquis* and promising himself that he would only formally tolerate the *yanqui* his sister inexplicably wished to marry. The *vaqueros,* however, were hopeful. There was word that the young señor who was to marry Señorita Antonia was no less than a United States marshal, and such a person must be much more ferocious than a mere sheriff, so that times would probably be better presently.

Meanwhile the Hacienda del Norte fared a little better than most of Dallas County. There was Don Luis, who had fought for the Confederacy, to turn the brown-skinned *vaqueros* into men who could fight otherwise than as individuals, helping each other as the members of even the smallest cavalry patrol use teamwork in combat for effectiveness. That helped. And there was a very old man at the hacienda named Carlos. He was a wrinkled ancient from down south near the border, and he had had vast and grim experience of the ways and tactics of banditry. The legend was that he had destroyed a famous bandit gang singlehanded, in years gone by. He taught the fine art of deciphering a trail, and the finer art of the lone-wolf destruction of bandits. This calculated instruction meant that the normal business of the hacienda was not carried out so efficiently, but it also meant that the dwindling of its longhorn herds grew less and less as time went on. It did not stop, but vigilance and an increasing efficiency in fighting paid off. Especially vigilance.

It was that organized vigilance which spotted Blayde Hollister and Weatherby—who had suddenly abandoned all reservations to his friendship with Blayde—when at long last they entered upon the range that belonged to the Hacienda del Norte. They did not know they had been sighted. That was old Carlos' training. They rode into a very neat ambush set for them according to the best of military principles. That was Don Luis' work. It was an admirably professional job, that ambuscade.

There was woodland on one side of where they rode, and a steep slope on the other side. Together, the obstacles closed in the way before them.

Blayde was amused. Weatherby was saying earnestly:
"I don't think you believe me a coward, Blayde. It's
simply that I am incompetent. I'm willing enough to risk
getting killed, if it will do any good, but that's the point.
What's needed is someone who can really do what I only
thought I could do with Marshal Hickok to help me.
It wouldn't have worked with him, though, and it
wouldn't have worked with you. As a figurehead I would
be useless. All the Marlows would need would be to kill
me, and any authority I delegated would be gone. So—"

Blayde said dryly, "It's what I suggested in Springfield. Me be the marshal and you be the deputy. Do you
want to swear me in?"

Weatherby said impatiently, "Swear? Why? I don't
even need your promise. I know you. What I want is
for you to agree to do the work."

"Since the Marlows seem to be the local ringleaders,"
said Blayde with a certain irony, "you couldn't stop me.
But I'll do it very formally for the United States government, ignoring the private quarrel of that government
with me. I'll even bear in mind what the government
would want."

"Apprehend the Marlows," said Weatherby urgently.
"That's the purpose. I was appointed for it. You do that
and—the government shouldn't be ungrateful."

"Speak for yourself," said Blayde. "Republics never are
grateful, especially to rebels who go and hold up their
officers after a war is over."

But he took the golden badge Weatherby held out to
him, and pinned it on his shirt. His lips crinkled a little
at their corners.

Then a voice cried harshly, "Halt!"

There was a simultaneous stirring all about them.
Rifle barrels appeared. The two riders had come to the
end of the clear land, which was a glade or perhaps
the meadow of a long vanished river. Their horses had
chosen as the easiest path a way between a steep brush-
covered slope and the edge of the woodland that barred
their view. Now, suddenly, the brushwood seemed fairly

to sprout gun barrels as a cactus sprouts spines. There were half a dozen weapons bearing ominously upon them.

The horses checked automatically. The guns steadied.

"The devil!" said Blayde, stiffening.

Weatherby's face turned obstinate. He said in a low tone, "Ready?"

"No!" snapped Blayde. "Don't try to draw. This is my fault. I should have been watching."

The same harsh voice said warningly, "You do not pass here. We do not weesh to keel, but—go back!"

Weatherby snapped, "We ride where we please."

"Hold it!" commanded Blayde. He said politely to the gun barrels, "We are looking for the Hacienda del Norte. The home of Don Felipe Robles. If he is your enemy—"

Casually, his hand dropped by his side. It was not a menacing move, but it made him much more ready for action than was apparent. Even his boots stirred slightly. He was ready for a sharp slash of the spurs, which would send Yank forward in a furious leap and draw the fire to himself while it spoiled all aiming.

There was a pause. Then a dark man thrust his head into view. He looked at Blayde and Weatherby with a vast suspicion.

"Thees ees the Hacienda del Norte," he said, examining them closely and without cordiality. "Strangers are not permitted to cross this land. There has been"—he spoke with formal but suspicious courtesy—"much rustleeng."

"You astonish me," said Blayde. "I have only come all the way here from Boston on account of it."

The dark man examined him more suspiciously still. "You are the *yanqui* marshal?"

"The name," said Blayde, "is Weatherby. I have pinned on my badge. I was about to begin active operations. Will you guide us to Don Felipe and Señorita Antonia?"

"Eef you speak truly," said the dark man, frowning, "you are mos' welcome. But there 'ave been many lies. You weel not touch your peestols. Thees way. You weel excuse us," he added coldly, "eef we take much care."

He led a horse out of the brushwood—the rifle barrels did not waver—and beckoned. He preceded them a short distance, and held up his hand. They paused again. There was a scrambling, and men mounted in their rear. They did not mount all at once. Some mounted, and when they were firmly in their saddles and their guns were handy again, the others mounted.

"Now," said the dark man. He slipped into his saddle and led the way. The cavalcade moved on.

"Somebody's trained these men," said Blayde appreciatively. "A good officer, too. I wonder who he is."

"Probably Antonia's brother," said Weatherby in a low tone. "Remember, you have to be me for everybody but Antonia."

"It may be awkward," objected Blayde.

"You have to have authority," insisted Weatherby. "Antonia told me about the servants. They'll take orders only from the boss. You don't want me to have to confirm every order you give. But that's the way they are."

Blayde frowned. "But the family—"

"For once," said Weatherby fiercely, "do something my way!"

They were suddenly out of close country where brush cut off the view. The dark man had served as advance guard for the whole party. Now that there was clear vision all around and an ambush was impossible, the man who had arranged an excellent ambush for Blayde and Weatherby dropped back to the two quasi prisoners.

"You weel understand," he said with ungracious politeness, "that we must be careful. Don Felipe has ordered the greatest caution. Only three days ago we found rustlairs at work and drove them away. Then came Señor Marlow—"

"Which?" snapped Blayde. Somehow the question was like a whip cracking.

"Señor Weel Marlow," said their guide distastefully. "He fired hees peestol and pretended to Don Felipe and Don Luis that he himself had aided to drive the rustlairs away. And as he spoke, keeping Don Felipe and Don Luis steel out of courtesy, there was a shot and a bullet came close to Don Luis. Almost eet keeled heem. Eenches only eet meesed. So we trust not anyone at all."

"It's about time I got here!" said Blayde. "They feel pretty smart. This Will Marlow, now—he's not known as an outlaw?"

"Known? *Sí!* But he pretends to be deeferent from hees brothairs. There ees no law here. He says he ees a banker. A beesinessman." The dark man added coldly, "Eef you are not what you say, you know all thees."

Blayde nodded. This was cagy politeness indeed. Courtesy that revealed nothing.

"A good officer trained you men," he observed. "I shall tell him so." Then he pointed. "That's the house?"

It was sprawling and picturesque from where they saw it. The whole hacienda dwelling was enclosed in a wall high enough to be a defense against any attackers un-equipped with artillery. There were watch towers at the corners, too, so that it had something of the aspect of a castle. But the great gateway did not open upon a moat, and from above they could see that the dwelling within was roofed with colored tiles, and that there was a gar-den, and the small bright tints of flowers could be seen. Sunlight glinted on a rifle barrel in one of the towers, though, and Blayde's approval was warm.

"If anybody'd be safe anywhere," he said, "it would be here. That's good!"

Weatherby was staring with all his eyes. They were startled, but they glowed—and yet that amazement re-mained. To a well-raised young man from Boston, it would be astonishing to find that this was the home of the young lady he had met in a Beacon Street residence, and had wooed and won in the most decorous of Boston fashions. But he drew a deep breath of satisfaction.

"It's very beautiful. I don't see how she can think of living in Boston after this."

The cavalcade rode down the long slant to the wall; Blayde and the dark man and Weatherby in front, and the men of the ambuscade behind. Blayde suddenly tapped the dark man on the arm.

"Your men are easing," he observed, "just because they are in sight of home. Somebody might take advantage of that someday."

The dark man looked behind and flushed. His followers were now distinctly riding at ease. Three of them had replaced their guns in the rifle holsters beside their saddles. He rasped an angry reproach at them, and then looked respectfully at Blayde.

"*Gracias, señor,*" he said. "I weel take note."

But he allowed himself a change in his manner.

They reached the house. They rode into the great courtyard and dismounted. There was a straight, dark-eyed man with silver hair standing upon the threshold of the great door. Weatherby whispered fiercely:

"To everybody but Antonia! Remember!"

Blayde nodded. The golden marshal's badge glittered on his shirt. He advanced. The dark man who had been their captor said respectfully:

"*Don Felipe, estos son extranjeros, pero se dicen que—*"

The stately man looked intently at Blayde. Then he stepped forward.

"Surely," he said in wholly unaccented English, "you are Martin?"

"So I am told, sir," said Blayde politely. "And you are Antonia's father. I am most happy."

He shook hands. A thin young man within the house regarded Blayde without approval.

"And let me present my son, Luis. Luis, this is Antonia's *novio,* Señor Martin Weatherby. You welcome him, of course."

Blayde moved forward with outstretched hand.

"There's been some sound military training going on around here," he said warmly. "I believe you're responsible?"

The thin young man ignored the offered hand under the excuse of bowing profoundly.

"Thank you," he said coldly. "Unfortunately, the late

war was not a war of soldiers alone, but of mechanics and factories. Otherwise it would have ended differently."

Blayde started, and the corners of his mouth quirked. That was his opinion also, of course. But in the eyes of young Luis Robles—and he saw the stiffened leg the young man tried to hide—he was Martin Weatherby, who was at least a Yankee from Boston, and might be a bragging victor.

"Luis!" said Don Felipe sharply. "You are discourteous to our guest—and to your future brother-in-law."

"I but stated, sir, what I believe is true," said the younger man coldly.

"There is much to be said for the view," Blayde interposed quickly. And again it was his own belief, but the young Texan took it for condescending kindness. His eyes flashed.

Don Felipe pointedly dismissed the matter, though angrily. He said politely to Blayde:

"And this gentleman?" He indicated the real Weatherby.

Weatherby squirmed. He'd had his own motives for insisting that even Antonia's family should think Blayde other than a defiant rebel and an outlaw—which to him meant a social outcast—but now he realized that the stately Don Felipe would be a difficult man to explain such a deception to afterward. He looked appealingly at Blayde.

"This"—Blayde's eyes crinkled—"this is my brother. He is—Daniel Weatherby." Weatherby advanced awkwardly to shake hands, and Blayde added gravely, "Daniel from the lion's den, you know."

Then there was a small movement some distance away. He looked through the long paneled hall from the entrance door to a great, high-ceilinged room. He saw a girl there. It was Antonia. He knew it instantly because she was smiling, and it was a warm and friendly and sweet smile, and Blayde abruptly knew that her every movement was bound to be infinitely graceful, and her voice clear and soft and quite unlike bells or flutes or anything but Antonia's voice, and Blayde understood just exactly how Weatherby had felt when he met her at a staid gathering on Beacon Street, in Boston.

"My house is yours," said Don Felipe to Weatherby. But he added to Blayde, "Antonia did not mention that you had a brother."

"We do not mention him—in Boston," said Blayde with gentle malice. "But we hope that in Texas even a black sheep—"

His eyes returned to Antonia, smiling at Weatherby. She had not heard a word, of course. But Blayde felt very complex emotions at the moment, in which the fact that this girl was promised to Weatherby figured largely. He resented it, and the deception in which Weatherby had involved him, and he was abruptly less than satisfied with an entire world in which a situation like this could exist.

He felt Weatherby growing faintly indignant. He knew that Antonia would come to greet her fiancé, and that the act would reveal everything, and that the intended deception would immediately seem a very cheap and shoddy thing. Don Felipe would not like it.

"Pardon," he said quickly, "but there is Antonia. If you permit me—"

He did not wait for permission. He went swiftly, as a lover should go, down the long hall toward her. He called eagerly, "Antonia!"

He was before her. He bent as if to kiss her, and whisked her out of the line of sight. She gasped in amazement. But he grinned at her ruefully.

"Quick!" he said urgently. "I'm pretending to be Martin. He will explain when he can. Play the part for a moment!"

She stared at him. He smiled at her warmly. And if she had known that the real Weatherby loved her even before he spoke to her, on Beacon Street, she surely saw that Blayde did not want her to dislike him.

"Please!" he said more urgently still. "I'll call him.

Just one instant—wait until he speaks!" He drew back from her and moved to where he could be seen down the long hallway. He smiled with every appearance of infinite happiness. "Daniel! Come here! I want you to meet Antonia!"

Then Weatherby came in and Antonia flew to him joyously.

"Antonia, my darling!" said Weatherby reverently.

"Martin!" But then she said breathlessly, "But Martin! What is this he has been telling me?"

Weatherby said formally, "Antonia, this is Blayde Hollister. Mr. Hollister, Señorita Antonia Robles."

Blayde bowed, his lips twitching. She looked from one to the other.

"But—but—why is he here?"

"To see that the Marlows are taken care of," said Weatherby hurriedly. "He is my deputy—or rather I am his. But it is important that *he* be known here as Martin Weatherby. Terribly important!"

"I do not understand."

"No one but you must know who he is. He has enemies, and you must trust him and let him pass for me."

"I hope soon to have fewer enemies," said Blayde, "and I promise that the hardship will not be for long."

The girl looked uncertainly from one to the other. Blayde saw with a very peculiar wrench in his heart that she was very fond indeed of Martin Weatherby. And he saw into Weatherby's heart by the honest, clumsy emotion that his face expressed. All of which annoyed Blayde Hollister horribly. But he heard footsteps approaching, which would be Don Felipe and the bitter, thin young man who was Antonia's brother.

"You must decide at once," said Blayde quickly, "and I am afraid Martin will not be in your father's good graces if you reveal him as deceitful so soon."

She looked uncertainly at the door, and at Martin Weatherby, and then very searchingly at Blayde. Then she said loyally:

"I am sure that you will explain later, Martin."

Her father entered the room, and Antonia smiled at him and said valiantly, "My father, you have met Martin, but I present him again. Mr. Martin Weatherby, who has done me the honor to ask me to be his wife."

And she reached out and put her hand in Blayde's.

Which would have been a very excellent beginning indeed, so Blayde reflected sardonically, if only it had happened to be true.

Late that night he paced up and down the really huge room that had been assigned to Weatherby and himself. The ceiling seemed extraordinarily high, and the walls were paneled in wood instead of plaster. The floor was stone and the bed a splendid carved affair, and there were hangings everywhere of stiff and ancient silk. Weatherby sat on the edge of the bed, making ready to retire.

"She is everything I said, isn't she?" he asked.

"My dear Martin," said Blayde restlessly, "you of all people should not criticize poets for their inability at description. Your account of the lady was a masterpiece of understatement."

He stared out of the window into the night.

"You can see, then," said Weatherby reverently, "why I would have defied my family for her if it had been necessary."

"Most men," said Blayde curtly, over his shoulder, "would defy not only parents but presidents and kings and perhaps even higher authorities for such a girl."

"Then you see why I didn't change my plans even when Hickok wouldn't fall in with them?"

Blayde turned his head. "You thought about it?"

Weatherby considered. "No." He seemed faintly surprised. "I was on my way to where I would see Antonia. It didn't occur to me that I could turn back, no matter what happened." Then he added meditatively, "It's odd. When it comes to Antonia I don't stop to think. I seem to know what is the right thing to do without thinking. I don't seem to need to think where she is concerned."

Blayde opened his mouth to speak, and closed it, and

stared out the window again. Presently he said with some irony:

"I'm not sure you have done the right thing. I have been presented to her family as you. There may be difficulties in your speaking to her freely, since you are believed to be only my brother."

"Oh, Antonia will arrange that," said Weatherby confidently. "And the Robles' aren't foreign. They aren't peculiar in their customs. They're as American as we are!"

"The family has even been a few centuries longer on the continent," agreed Blayde with the same effect of irony. "But I am afraid they will not be pleased when they learn that you introduced a known outlaw, a wanted man—someone they will consider a scoundrel—into their house."

"Luis considers you a scoundrel now," said Weatherby with a grin, "because he thinks you're me, and I'm a Yankee. Do you think he'd dislike you so poisonously if he knew you were Colonel Reb Hollister?"

"Who," said Blayde quietly, "is dead."

"Who," said Weatherby, "might come alive again under proper conditions."

Again Blayde jerked his head around to stare at Weatherby in the light of the fat candles that gave light to this room.

"After the Marlows are taken care of," said Weatherby, "that might be taken up. My family has some influence, Blayde."

Blayde whirled. His face was set and angry.

"Listen to me!" he said hotly. "I did not undertake this affair for pay, and you know it! I came here to find and kill the Marlows. It is a personal matter between the Marlows and myself. I cannot be paid for killing them. I will not accept pay for killing them, either in money or in any other way. If your family tries to reward me with the use of their influence, for the use of my pistols to kill the Marlows, I promise that you and they will regret it! I am not for hire to kill anyone!"

Weatherby almost gasped in shocked apology. "I didn't mean that, Blayde!"

"Then don't say it," snapped Blayde. "Don't think it! I asked questions about the Marlows at dinner and afterward. One of them pretends to respectability. He has actually had the cold nerve to set up in business as a banker—by seeing to it that a Dallas banker was killed by an 'unknown' assassin and purchasing his business, his mortgages and the like, from the widow. He owns a heavy loan upon the Hacienda del Norte, caused by the loss of cattle to his rustling brothers. He used the result of the gang's lootings back home for capital. Now he uses his brothers—they, if you please, are outlaws, but he is not!—to make riches more cleverly than by merely stealing. When they steal, they create a predicament of which their now-banker brother makes use. Then they act to let him take over what they first caused to be put in pawn!"

Weatherby stared at him, with one boot in his hand.

"You mean he's in *business*," he asked incredulously, "and uses his outlaw brothers to help his *business*?"

Blayde grimaced. "Rustling, robbery, and murder are the business. Banking transactions with Will Marlow are just the means by which such doings pay double. He pretends to fear and despise his brothers. He deplores that they are such violent men. But everything they do turns out to his profit. And if something can profit him, they do it!"

"I thought," said Weatherby blankly, "that they were just ordinary thieves and murderers."

Blayde shrugged. "They're ordinary in that a bullet will kill them the same as anybody else. I'm riding into the town of Dallas in the morning. If I could catch the three of them together, I could end it at once. But I don't want one of them running away, to be hunted all over again. I shall lay my plans."

Weatherby suddenly grinned. "You remember the town of Callao?"

Blayde frowned.

"The story got here before us," said Weatherby.
"United States Marshal Weatherby, who came on a bandit gang in possession of a trail herd and a town together
and wiped them out—he has a reputation in Dallas. Don
Felipe told me that he was sure I was proud of my
brother."

Blayde scowled. "Well?"

"They may be afraid of you. They may walk warily.
Blayde, I've every confidence you're going to handle
this affair. But—really, Blayde, you ought to think of
the future after it. I mean that! There's no reason for
your future to be as black as you seem to think."

Weatherby peeled. He was a skinny naked figure in
the stately bedroom. He got into a nightshirt that had
been in his saddlebags ever since he had scrapped his
Gladstone bag, because of its hopeless inappropriateness
for a man on horseback. His head popped through the
top of the garment.

"It feels good," he said blithely, "to get properly un-
dressed to sleep. I feel very good about everything, Blayde.
My future looks bright. I'd like to feel that yours was,
too."

"You wouldn't wish me as beautiful a girl as Antonia
to marry, would you?" asked Blayde sardonically.

"As nice a one, yes," said Weatherby. He said suddenly, "I think you and Martha Farquehar would hit it
off well. You're both rather wonderful people, and you've
both been friends to me. I'd like you to meet Martha."

Then Blayde grinned at him. The anger and the irony
went out of his manner. Weatherby was inept. He was
clumsy. He was not perceptive and he was not clever—
but he was not suspicious, either. And he was an honest
man inside.

"You're sort of a fool, Martin, and I like you for it,"
said Blayde gently. "But that sort of thing is not in the
cards for me. Hickok said it. As Reb Hollister I had a
reputation I didn't wholly earn. On the way down here,
you tell me, I got a new reputation I didn't really earn,
either. Anybody could have smashed that raid on Callao.

When I've taken care of the Marlows, I'll probably have another reputation on top of that. And it will mean that any man who kills me will be famous. So no braggart or fool will feel he is a really bad man unless he's faced me in a pistol duel. I'll have to learn to sit with my back always against a wall. I'll have to learn never to relax so I can't reach a pistol quicker than any other man around me. I'll have to learn never to let anyone get behind me. And I'll have to kill men I have no quarrel with, just to keep them from killing me. And I won't know why!"

Weatherby shook his head. "I'll talk it over with Antonia," he said with confidence. "We have to plan to tell her father about you eventually, anyhow. She'll think of something."

Blayde turned away. There was moonlight tonight, and this window looked out upon the garden and the blooms within the wall surrounding the Hacienda del Norte. He looked out at the night and the flowers that Antonia walked among sometimes.

Hickok had said it. With the murderers he had hunted so long at last within his reach—certainly closer than he'd ever had them before—he knew that the town marshal of Springfield had been right. He'd said that Blayde had been left with nothing but his family by the death of the Confederacy, and nothing but an obligation to kill three men when his family died. When that obligation was liquidated, his life would be absolutely empty. Until now, Blayde hadn't believed it.

Now he knew it was so. Before he met Antonia, he couldn't imagine a life he would want to live. He couldn't picture a life he would want to build. Now he could. But Weatherby would be the man to live and build it, in happiness and contentment, through long years of life with Antonia.

Under the circumstances, Blayde told himself dryly that the best thing that could possibly happen would be for him to get himself killed in the act of killing the last of the Marlow brothers. If he didn't, he would be rather more than likely to fulfill the least optimistic of Wild Bill's predictions. He didn't want to be a target for self-proclaimed bad men seeking reputations as killers. He didn't want that reputation for himself. But it had gravitated to him twice.

With nothing in the world that he could both want and have, Blayde stared out into the night and made plans for as far as he could imagine into the future. It was not far.

Chapter Seven

THE WORLD moved on with no particular interest in Dallas County. The newspapers remarked indignantly upon the conferring of a cardinal's hat upon Lucien Bonaparte, a grandson of Napoleon's younger brother. The Union Pacific Railroad had reached a point six hundred miles west of Omaha, Nebraska. The steamer *Sea Bird* burned in Lake Michigan, with a loss of ninety-seven lives out of one hundred persons on board. The billiard championship of America was settled by a match between John McDevitt and Joseph Dion, McDevitt winning by a run of 1,460, which was the longest run then recorded as made on a billiard table. There was an earthquake at St. Thomas, West Indies, accompanied by a remarkable tidal wave. In the Sandwich Islands the volcano Mauna Loa was in eruption, and at one time the earthquake shocks were so violent that not one living creature on the island was able to stand on its feet. The Kentucky election case was decided in the House of Representatives in favor of Samuel McKee, a Unionist, over Judge Young, a former Secessionist. The new queen of Madagascar abolished idol worship in her dominions. Train robbers seized the engine and express car of a train at Seymour, Indiana, killed the express messenger, drove the engine to where their horses waited, and escaped with $40,000. Time and progress together marched on.

Blayde rode in to Dallas in the morning. He was grimly silent. He realized that his original, simple purpose had become involved with other matters. If he had come down to Texas alone and riding fast, as soon as he'd heard of the Marlows' whereabouts, he'd have been untrammeled now. He would be riding into Dallas, alone and purposefully, to kill William Marlow. Then he would have had only to hunt down the other two of the brothers, kill them, and he would be through. But then what?

94

Hickok had analyzed it accurately. He'd had nothing to
live for but the Confederacy and his family, and both
were dead, but they'd left him a legacy of vengeance to
be satisfied. When that was done, he'd have faced complete emptiness. Now he had other obligations.

Weatherby was one. He'd been taken on as a com-
panion because he had been resolved on a program that
would inevitably have got him killed. This present role
of United States marshal had been adopted partly to
protect him, though partly as a reasonable aid in pin-
pointing his quarry. People would give information to
a United States marshal when they might fear to talk
too much to a mere stranger. But that role, in turn, had
led to his meeting Antonia.

And now he had an obligation there. It was not based
on reason but on the fact that she was the one woman
he would have chosen to spend the rest of his life with
—had the choice been possible. She amounted to the
one purpose that he could have taken on in following
Hickok's advice to choose another purpose and devote
his life to it. But she was an impossible purpose. Yet
she was an obligation, because it is the instinct of a man
to serve and protect and somehow cherish some one
woman, and Antonia needed what he could do.

Antonia was guarded, to be sure. But when she married Weatherby she would again be exposed to the dan-
gers that had most women in Texas equipped with derringers for their personal safety. And those derringers
were used.

Weatherby rode silently at Blayde's side. Blayde
thought of him with something of irritation, and yet he
would not have canceled his recent actions had it been
possible. He would not willingly let go having met
Antonia.

There were trees here, oak and ash and pecan and
sycamore. The ground was fertile. It would be cotton
country if ever a way of sending cotton to the market
should appear. Now there were some cattle; not too
many, and all longhorns and nothing else. There were

a few homesteaders in the county, but though the need
to carry a rifle while plowing was not absolute as in the
Indian days, it was not at all foolish. So there was not
much agriculture in Dallas County.

They saw the town before them. There were tree-
shaded streets. They would be unpaved, of course. Street
paving was a boast of cities in the East—and for their
principal streets only. Dallas sprawled, and there were
a corral and livery stable and stores. There was even
a three-story building, the flour mill. Altogether it was
very much more than a backwoods settlement. It was
a very tiny city. There were drooping cow ponies before
its saloons, to be sure, but there were as many wagons
moving along upon their lawful occasions.

Blayde and Weatherby rode into the town. It was
notable that here there were women in plain view, and
that they were not slovenly. They were crisply dressed.
If many of their gowns were homespun cotton, there was
still a thought of fashion as well as of modesty. There
were men in the dress of citizens, wearing no arms. Perhaps more significant still, the houses did not appear to
have been erected in feverish haste, and there was glass
in all the windows. There was no single substitution of
oiled paper for a windowpane.

They went on. It seemed strange to Blayde to ride
into a town where people appeared to have lived for a
number of years. The backwoods settlements of Missouri
had all looked improvised. The few small hamlets on the
way down from Springfield had looked essentially tem-
porary. But here was a town in which it was unreason-
able that life and property should not be safe. This was a
substantial town of substantial people.

They reached the section where the stores and saloons
seemed to have gathered. There was the Dallas Feed and
Grain Company. There was the Dallas *Herald* office.
There was the Dallas Bank. Swinging wooden signs valiantly claimed the status of civilization.

Then Blayde saw the sign he had been looking for from
the moment he entered the town:

WM. MARLOW AND COMPANY
Land Bought and Sold
Mortgages — Insurance

There was another line under it. "Successors to—" But
that was smudged and obliterated.

Weatherby caught his breath. "There's one of the Marlows," he said. "You'll arrest him?"

"I'll get him," said Blayde. "But he's the smart one,
remember. I want all three. The one called Bryant is the
one who carried off and killed my sister. I want him first."

He looked down at his hands. Their knuckles were
white. He deliberately relaxed them. He deliberately
loosened all the muscles in his body. They had gone tense
at this evidence that he was near the end of his mission.

"First I want to make sure of a few things," said Blayde.
"It's not good tactics to launch an attack unless you know
what you're going to run up against."

"We'll go to the newspaper office, then," said Weatherby. "That's where the news is found."

"We'll have a drink," Blayde told him. "The newspaper prints only a discreet part of what its editor hears
in saloons."

He reined in at the Chuckaway Saloon. He dismounted
and fastened Yank's reins to the hitching rail. Weatherby
said suddenly:

"I've wondered, Blayde. Why do you tie your reins in
that sort of knot?"

"I can untie it in a hurry," said Blayde briefly, "if I
ever need to leave fast."

Weatherby painstakingly imitated Blayde's knot.

They entered the saloon. Again it was different. Most
of the saloons between Springfield and Texas had simply
been places where a man could get a drink fast. Sometimes there was gambling attached. The taxes on saloons
and gambling houses helped maintain most of the public-
school systems west of the Mississippi. Such places were
furnished with some luxury. But mostly saloons were

merely barrel shops where one could get a drink, or several, and call it a day. This one, though, was well fitted out and there was a mirror back of the bar, and even sawdust on the floor. The last was possible because there were three sawmills in the county. One had been held up three times in six months for its payroll, and debated closing down.

The men in this saloon, though, were much like men in other saloons elsewhere. A cowboy with his hat tilted far back on his head lifted his glass with great caution and put it carefully to his lips. The conscious precision paid off. He did not spill a drop. In the back of the saloon, somebody got painstakingly to his feet, got deliberately set for the effort, and let out a shrill yell.

"Ya-hoo-o-o-o-o! I'm a wildcat! I can lick any man in the place! I'm r'arin'!"

He glared about him. A chunky man, plainly the owner of the saloon, went methodically over to him, steadied him by a hand on one shoulder, and knocked smartly at the back of his knee with the other hand. The defiant one sat down abruptly in the chair behind him.

The chunky man went back behind the bar. He approached Blayde and Weatherby. "Yep, gents?"

Blayde ordered. Weatherby looked fascinatedly at the man who had been sat down.

"Does he do that often?" he asked.

"Yes," said the proprietor matter-of-factly. "About every three drinks after the first couple. Seems to get a lot of satisfaction out of it. He's about due to go to sleep now."

He served them.

"You're strangers," he observed.

Blayde nodded. "At the moment. My name's Weatherby."

The Chuckaway's proprietor looked at him a second time. His eyes fell on the golden badge, provided by Weatherby's admiring family.

"You the new marshal?" At Blayde's nod he said, "Good! We been expectin' you. Excuse me."

He ducked under a part of the bar and went out the door. In a moment or two he came back.

"People you'd ought to meet," he explained. "Things are right bad heah. They'll be heah in a minute."

"I've been hearing that things are bad," admitted Blayde. "In what way?"

The Chuckaway's proprietor said detachedly, "Rustlin', partly. Killin's, partly. Mostly not knowin' who's likely to shoot you in the back. A man can take care of himself if he knows who's gunnin' for him. He guns first. But in this town you disapprove of one fella and first thing you know somebody else blows your head off from the dark, an' the first guy you don't like is playin' cards public at the time."

Blayde said, "Somehow, I don't think that's true of many people. Just a certain number it's dangerous to disapprove of. Maybe only one or two. Right?"

"That's right," said the proprietor of the Chuckaway. "But you got to make your own guess as to who that is. I'm not talkin'."

The door darkened. Two men came in. One was a bulky man with "cattleman" written all over him. The other was a rock-jawed smaller elderly man in city clothing. The Chuckaway's owner nodded in their direction.

"Judge Harper," he said briefly. "Federal court. And Matt Coulter. Bar W. Gentlemen, this's Marshal Weatherby."

The dour-faced older man looked estimatingly at Blayde, and nodded. "How-do, Marshal. Been expecting you for some days. You're needed."

The cattleman looked at Blayde and his brows contracted. "Weatherby? Did you say your name was Weatherby?"

Blayde's face grew flinty. "Why the question?"

"Seems to me like I've seen you somewheres," said Coulter slowly, "and not in this kinda getup. Seems like it was a uniform."

"And me from Boston?" asked Blayde dryly. But his face did not relax.

"No-o-o-o," agreed Coulter. "That ain't likely. If I saw any Yanks during the war, it was down a musket barrel." He shook hands. "I guess I got a wrong idea. But we heard about you, suh. It's been good hearin'. And if you haul in the scalawags, Judge Harper'll jail 'em!"

The Judge said with asperity, "When the evidence warrants it, Mr. Coulter!"

"Evidence, hell!" growled Coulter. "Everybody knows it's the Marlows are back of nine tenths of the hell-raisin' that goes on!"

"Nobody's come forward to testify who's actually seen them break the law!" snapped the Judge. "That's what the Federal court will go by!"

Coulter turned to Weatherby. "And you, suh?"

"My brother," interposed Blayde. "And my deputy."

Coulter looked him up and down. He obviously compared him with Blayde.

"Looks spindlin' to me," he observed. "No offense, suh."

Blayde saw a look of obstinacy beginning to form on Weatherby's face. He said:

"That hat he's wearing was Wild Bill Hickok's. He shot it off Wild Bill's head. Bill's initials are in the hat band. That's why I brought him along. Keep him out of trouble."

The faces of those about Weatherby changed. They were respectful, very respectful. He was embarrassed.

The Judge cleared his throat. "Marshal Weatherby, suh," he said firmly, "I told you we are glad you are here. But if you make arrests, they will come up in my court. And my court is run by the statutes. This is not—" his mouth pursed disapprovingly—"this is not the wild West. This district is facing east and it is East, and wild-West disregard for law will not be tolerated."

Somewhere in the street outside the saloon a sudden drum roll of explosions sounded, as if someone were fanning a pistol. In the middle of the rat-tat-tat there was a single other explosion. Then there was silence.

Blayde was among the first to get out of the saloon.

Others followed, and still others appeared after having ducked out of the way when bullets began to fly. There was a man lying in the street, an emptied Colt not far from his hand. On the sidewalk, painstakingly reloading a Confederate Army pistol, there was another man in dusty garments. A tired, drooping horse stood nearby. Judge Harper bustled over.

"What's this?" he snapped. "What the hell's this?"

The man in dusty clothes looked up levelly. "Him," he said heavily, "he was over to Dos Almas a couple of weeks ago. He picked a fight with my kid brother. The kid whaled the tar outa him. He went an' got on his hawss, came ridin' up to the kid, shot him five times, an' rid off. I found out he'd joined up with Cullen an' Bryant Marlow, an' I rode over here. Just now I saw him walkin' by, and I called him, an' he saw an' recognized me. He started fannin' his pistol, an' I killed him."

There was a murmur of agreement. No less than half a dozen men who had appeared from behind walls and inside doors after the shooting stopped now nodded their agreement.

"Dammit," said Judge Harper, "we can't have this sort of thing! But he shot first?"

Three or four voices chimed in:

"Yeah."

"Sure did!"

"I saw it, Judge. That's right!"

Judge Harper scowled, turning his eyes sternly.

"Any kin to you?" he demanded of one man. "You?" he demanded again as the first man shook his head. "You? Did this man make any threats?"

Somebody said, "All he said was 'You there, I been looking for you!' Then that fella"—he indicated the body in the road—"he saw him and turned kinda green an' started pumpin' lead."

"To say that you have been looking for a man is not a threat in the eyes of the law," said Judge Harper irritably. "If the dead man shot first, then he was the aggressor. A man's entitled to defend himself. Dammit!

Dammit! There's nothing to be done." The Judge turned angrily to Blayde. "Marshal, if you arrest this man, any jury will acquit him. There's no sense in bothering with it."

"I'm inclined to agree with you, sir," said Blayde gravely. He turned to the dusty man. "You won't be staying in town, I take it?"

"I did what I came for," the man said levelly.

Blayde suddenly jerked out a pistol and fired. Glass crashed in a window of the offices of William Marlow. A rifle fell out of that window to the ground. It exploded smokily as it hit the earth.

Blayde stood still, facing the window, his legs apart, his pistol held ready, his nostrils distended. Men scattered from about him. He stood alone in the dusty street, a fair target with the bright sunshine on him. But he was deadly.

After seconds he said over his shoulder to the dusty man, "Maybe you'd better get started back home now. I'll see they don't come after you."

The dusty man said quietly, "He'd joined up with Cullen and Bryant. I reckon they figured on getting me for killing him. They'll prob'ly try again. But he murdered my kid brother without givin' him a chance."

"I'll try to give them something else to do," said Blayde.

He watched the window. Just then a man came riding down the street. Coulter, the cattleman, swore in a growling voice.

"There's Will Marlow now! He wasn't in there! He's never where anything happens, damn him!"

Blayde looked for the first time at one of the three brothers he had trailed so grimly and so earnestly. This Marlow was a grossly fat man, with hard muscle underneath the fat. He reined in at sight of the tableau.

"Mr. Marlow," snapped the Judge acidly, "there was a shooting here. One of your brothers' friends got killed —and then somebody poked a rifle out of your office window. Mr. Marlow, you go up into your office and chase whoever is in it down here for me to get a look at him!"

The fat man swelled with seeming indignation.

"Those no-account brothers of mine makin' trouble again? They're a great trial to me, Judge! I'll go up there and chase 'em out! You fuss with 'em, Judge! I've argued with 'em and it ain't no use!"

Blayde reholstered his pistol with a jerk. He felt himself gone strangely pale. But he stood still. Then he said with a careful precision:

"Maybe I'd better go up there and search the office. Mr. Marlow might get hurt."

"Nothing of the kind, sir!" snapped the Judge. "It ain't any use! Dammit, either there's four or five of 'em in that office, or there ain't a single one! And what would a jury convict 'em for, when we can't prove which one was pointing that gun, and they didn't fire a shot anyway? But Marshal Weatherby, sir, I'm pleased with you. I think you are the kind of United States marshal this town needs."

But Blayde was watching as the fat man climbed the flight of outside stairs leading up to the office of Wm. Marlow and Company, Land Bought and Sold, Mortgages, Insurance. Seconds later Will Marlow's head appeared at the window with the smashed glass.

"Ain't a soul heah!" he bellowed. "But the back window's open!"

Judge Harper stamped his foot.

"Marshal," he said sternly, "you come back to the Chuckaway and have a talk with me."

Blayde hesitated a long time, eying the window with the bullet-smashed glass pane.

"There ain't anybody there!" repeated the Judge peevishly. "I know what I'm talking about! Maybe we can get something started to make things run the way they ought to, instead of the way they do."

Blayde set his teeth. He obeyed. One of the three men he had come so far to find was only across the street. The others might be there. But he had not come so far to make a blunder. He followed the Judge into the saloon again.

"A quick eye," said the Judge snappishly, "and a quick shot. It's a disgrace they were needed! Marshal Weatherby, you and me, we have to clean up this town. In a strictly legal way, Marshal! That's the only way it'll stay cleaned up. This town belongs with the East. It's not the West. Wild-West business can't be allowed here. Now, how is it going to be stopped?"

Blayde said quietly, "It can be done. But from what I hear, the first thing needed is for me to kill the Marlows or run them out."

"No!" snapped the Judge. "Maybe you can do it. Maybe you'll have to. But it'll be a tragedy if you do. The only way this town can be cleaned up so it'll stay cleaned up is if the citizens kill or run out those Marlow boys. You see that?"

Blayde listened, but his lips were set. He meant to handle the Marlows alone.

"Suppose one man did clean up this town, wild-West fashion," fumed the Judge. "What'd happen after? In time he'd go away. Then what'd happen? Some other damned scoundrels would come in and set up shop. Marshal, it's up to you and me to stir up these citizens so they'll tend to such things for themselves. Right now they're scared to say a word against the Marlows—even Cullen and Bryant. That's got to be stopped! You've made a good showing today. With you to lead them, the citizens of this town will show spunk. Lead them to a cleanup, instead of doing it all yourself, and the time will come when they'll tell you they don't need you any more. They'll tell you to clear out. You can make Dallas chase you out for doing your duty—and when you can do that, your duty's done!"

Blayde raised his eyebrows.

"I'd rather have quick action," he said dryly. Then he stiffened. Weatherby had just come in from the street. He nodded casually to Blayde.

"I went up into the Marlow office," he observed. "Nobody there but Will Marlow. He offered me a drink. It was very bad whisky."

He leaned against the bar. Blayde seethed. While he returned meekly to the saloon, Weatherby had gone up ready to do murder only a little while ago.

"You could have got killed!" snapped Blayde.

"I didn't," said Weatherby cheerfully.

"While you're my deputy," Blayde rasped, "you won't go risking getting shot for nothing! Nobody doubts your nerve! But I doubt your sense!"

Weatherby grinned a little. He said meekly, "Yes, Brother Martin."

Blayde glared at him. Then he turned to Judge Harper.

"I want to do things right," he said coldly, "and if your citizens are willing to do their part, I'll surely let them. But they've got to do their part or I'll handle it alone!"

The words were hardly out of his mouth before there was a highly distinctive sound some distance away. It was a volley of gunfire, a ragged blasting of several weapons at once.

Without a word, Blayde went out the saloon door again. Weatherby was with him instantly. Other men were crowding out into the street from other places. All stared in one direction.

Blayde swung on Yank and rode where the eyes turned, without realizing that his first action was to loosen his pistols in their holsters as he reached the saddle, and his second to cast a chilly glance up at the window whose glass he had smashed only ten minutes or so before.

There had been a normal number of people in sight about the houses—children, a woman weeding in a garden, and a man or two moving from one place to another. But now there was not a human being in sight save the men watching curiously from the Chuckaway and the other business places nearby.

The two horses' hoofs made a thudding noise on the powdery dust. There were no others in motion anywhere. There were other horses, and certainly plenty of men to form a posse, but the two rode alone. Blayde said:

"The local people aren't too anxious to step forward."

Weatherby said blithely, "This town stays treed, eh?"

"A little military knowledge," said Blayde grimly, "is a dangerous thing for a bushwhacker to have. Given spies to watch and report, and a good hideout to raid from, a gang of guerrillas can hold down a pretty big territory. They're simply using here the strategy they learned and used in the war. But there's a strategy of reply to that, too. There!"

There was a drooping, dusty horse standing in the road. There was a man, toppled from its saddle. Blayde glanced quickly and comprehensively around. He dismounted and turned the fallen man over. He knew the prone man was dead, of course. At least four bullets had plowed into his back. And he wasn't surprised to see who the man was.

It was the man from Dos Almas who, ten minutes or maybe fifteen minutes since, had shot it out with the murderer of his brother within fifty yards of the Chuckaway Saloon. He'd been murdered with a volley from behind for having won a perfectly fair pistol fight. His murderers had vanished. Blayde turned white with anger as he stared all around him again.

"Pretty smart," he said curtly.

Weatherby moved his horse here and there, looking for tracks. There were plenty of tracks. Too many tracks. It was impossible to tell which were those of the killers. Weatherby said uncomfortably:

"How are we going to trail them, Blayde?"

"Trail who?" asked Blayde sardonically. "And how would we know when we caught them?" He added abruptly, "Stay here with the body. I'll send somebody to look after things. Then wait in the Chuckaway for me. I'm going to have a little talk with Will Marlow."

"You mean—arrest him?"

"For what?" asked Blayde, again sardonically. "He wasn't in his office when somebody tried to kill this man before. He was in his office when this man was killed. And what else would I arrest him for? I'm going up to his office either to kill him or to set his brothers on that little task. He's the only one of the three that I'd recognize if I saw them on the street. I've got to be able to know the others in order to kill them. You wait here."

There was a great silence as Blayde rode alone back down the dusty street. There were men in sight around the clustered stores. They looked at Blayde as he rode into view. He stared coldly straight ahead. He was raging inside, not only at the infuriating knowledge that he was close to the three Marlow brothers, whose death he told himself was the primary purpose of his life, but also at the sheer effrontery of the happening just past. A man had killed a member of the Marlow gang in fair fight, before Will Marlow's office. Instantly it had been the intention of the gang to murder him for daring to take vengeance for a murder by one of their number. A bullet from Blayde's pistol stopped that first attempt. But the men who had certainly been in Will Marlow's office, and certainly had not come out of it down the stairs, were so brazen that their thought was not that of abandoning the intended murder, but of carrying it out immediately in some other way. And they had done so. It was insolence of a sort that would either be utterly terrifying or utterly infuriating.

Dallas County was under the thumb of an outlaw crew who had its citizens completely intimidated. They could resent, but not fight. They could not even organize to fight, because the first man to dream of gathering others to help oppose the Marlows would be reported by a Marlow spy and shot down by Marlow murderers. It had actually been intended to kill this man while he talked to a United States marshal. He had been killed in a manner that was not only defiance but mockery of the law. Blayde Hollister had had his troubles with the law—especially law as administered by occupation authorities in Valdosta, Georgia—but this derision was too much.

He did not look at the men in the street because he was angry enough to be ashamed of them. He rode to the Chuckaway Saloon and dismounted without letting his eyes rest on any individual. He tied Yank to the hitching rail. He turned his eyes to Judge Harper. He said without intonation:

"They killed that man from Dos Almas. Shot him in the back. You might send somebody down to get his body, unless you mean to leave it lying in the street."

He turned away. He walked across the street. He walked under the sign that hung at the foot of a flight of outside stairs leading to Will Marlow's second-story office. He mounted the stairs. He vanished under the roof that followed the stairway down to the street.

Judge Harper stamped his foot.

"Dammit!" he sputtered. "He's acting like this was the wild West! I won't have the law flouted! If he arrests Will Marlow and don't have evidence against him—"

Nobody paid the least attention. Every man stared across the street at the building in which Will Marlow had an office. Everyone believed him the brains of the outlaws who dominated Dallas County. Even Judge Harper suddenly stopped his fuming as time seemed to run out. He waited irritably.

It was a long time before anything happened. It was nearly three minutes before a roll of gunfire came echoing out of the office.

Chapter Eight

THE EXPRESSION Blayde wore when he crossed the street to Will Marlow's office was one that was long overdue in Dallas. The town had been a frontier outpost at first, and then a staid market town for the bigger ranches like the Hacienda del Norte, and then the war came and many of its younger men were killed in futile defense of the Confederacy, and Reconstruction followed. Then it seemed that the whole state would fall apart into chaotic, ungovernable sections, and Dallas was only one of many to go back to the lawlessness of an earlier time. With so many of what should have been its fighting men dead on faraway battlefields, and with Yankee-loving Governor Davis in the statehouse in Austin, troublous times were bound to come. And they were here. They were times in which it seemed that there was no special use in any effort at all.

The men Blayde left behind him looked ashamed, which was a good thing. Some of them looked angry, which was a better thing. But all of them only watched as Blayde put his foot on the bottom step under the sign, and as he climbed the stairs with deliberate lack of haste until he was hidden by the slanting roof that went down to the street level with the stairway.

He reached the landing at the head of the stairs. He heard faint, confused sounds within the building. Somebody was hurriedly giving orders inside there. Before they could be completed, Blayde stepped within.

It was not a suitable office for the head of an outlaw gang. Will Marlow had acquired it legally, with the assets and the business of a dead man. He had made this a definite step in his planning. Before it had come other steps. Killings marked most of those way points on his progress toward a bandit-based, law-protected dominion that was actually the object of his ambition. Men who stood in his way got killed, or else vanished and their killing was to be assumed even when their bodies were never discovered. This office had been taken over only after he was quite sure the county was intimidated, which was made possible by the fact that most men were already sick with defeat and personal grief and unrelieved disaster due to the war. So it had been quite practical to arrange that a prominent businessman of Dallas should run into a load of buckshot as he walked up the steps of his own front porch, and afterward it was practical to make a deal with his widow. She could not carry on the business. With Will Marlow bidding for it, nobody else would try. So the oldest of the three Marlows became an outwardly respectable businessman, and the reign of terror his brothers conducted was reorganized to be more secure and more profitable than ever before.

But Blayde went into the office and stood still, his nostrils flaring a little, his lips very taut, ready for instant and very much desired battle.

There was only one man in sight, though. Will Marlow himself, grossly fleshed, sat at ease before the desk the former owner of this office had brought by wagon all the way from Galveston.

He looked up and feigned surprise as Blayde looked to him ominously. There was a door in this room, leading somewhere to the rear. It had undoubtedly been from the room behind the door that the faint noises had come.

"Why—why—howdy, suh!" said Will Marlow with a fine air of cordiality. "I reckon you're Marshal Weatherby, suh. I heard you were comin'. First we heard it was Marshal Hickok who was supposed to come down here—an' sorely needed, too!"

Blayde paused a moment. His eyes burned a little, because this was one of three men he must kill. But he said levelly:

"No. Hickok didn't come. He's not doing peace-officer work any more. He's fired his last shot for the law."

Will Marlow blinked. "He got drilled?"

"There may have been a story to that effect," Blayde

said. "He fought it out with a man named Hollister."

Will Marlow tensed. "Hollister? Would that be Colonel Reb Hollister?"

Blayde nodded. His hands were close to his holsters. His eyes seemed fixed upon Will Marlow, but he was infinitely aware of all his surroundings. There was no one else in this room, but the door to the back was ever so slightly ajar, and there was somebody in there.

"Yes. That's the man," said Blayde. "They fought it out just outside the hotel in Springfield, Missouri. You knew Hollister?"

"Only by hearsay," said Will Marlow. He licked his lips. "And he drilled Marshal Hickok? Where is he? Talk, man!"

"Where's Hickok? He's retired. On his way east to do some play-acting. The fight with Hollister was his last official act as a peace officer."

"What happened in the fight?"

"Oh, Hollister got killed," said Blayde.

"Hollister's dead? By Gawd, that's good news! I'm goin' to uncork some bonded on that!" He dragged a bottle from a drawer of the desk. "Marshal Weatherby, suh, we'll have a drink to Wild Bill."

His hands shook. He poured into a glass, spilling pungent-smelling whisky.

"This isn't a social call," said Blayde coldly. "Judge Harper called to your attention, Mr. Marlow, that some-body pushed a rifle out of the front window of this office. He apparently intended to kill a man from Dos Almas who'd just had a duel with one of your brothers' friends —a fair fight—and killed him."

Marlow jerked his eyes to Blayde. Then he gulped down his drink. He wiped his mouth.

"That's bad, Marshal Weatherby. That's right bad! Those two brothers of mine are a cross and a tribulation. They're two black sheep in a fine family, Marshal. I've argued with them—"

Blayde said politely, "You know I know better than that, Mr. Marlow. They work for you."

Will Marlow looked shocked. Blayde heard a very faint sound in the next room. Without warning, he moved to one side. He ceased to be silhouetted against the open door. He smiled very faintly and very grimly.

"I'm sure you'll deny that," he said softly. "But I'll give you a chance to prove that you're opposed to the way they act. Will you tell me where to find them?"

Will Marlow's eyes turned ugly. "What for, Marshal? You got any evidence against them?"

"No," said Blayde. "But I'd hardly expect them to submit to arrest. Not without fighting."

"Now look, Marshal!" protested Will Marlow. "If things was different, and if they was popular around heah, and if they was goin' to be faced with their accusers an' have a fair trial, I'm not the man to stay in the way of the law, even if they are my own kith an' kin. But they're reckless boys, Marshal. They might start fightin'. And I cain't risk that."

Blayde was infinitely aware of every sound that there was in the world. Somewhere in the town a hen cackled, and somewhere very far away a wagon moved with a squeaky wheel, and there was a far-distant woman's voice, and the shuffling, scuffling noise of cow ponies outside the Chuckaway Saloon across the way. The men over there were wholly silent. But a board creaked in the back office here.

"I'm planning," said Blayde, "to arrange for everything you say you want—fair trial and all the rest. But right now you and your brothers have everybody afraid to speak. I'm going to call a mass meeting of citizens and put the situation to them. I'm going to rouse the county against the Marlow gang. Which," he added, "is you and your brothers. Of course, I might not be able to hold the assembled citizens in line, once they get started. They might want to start lynching."

He waited for sounds that would indicate that whoever was in the next room was disturbed. There was no sign.

"I'm thinking of settling here," added Blayde untruthfully, adding temptation to the threat, "and I'm willing to put some money in the town. I hope to buy a building for a town hall and give it to the city of Dallas. Nobody knows it but you. Nobody else knows that I've got ten thousand dollars in greenbacks on me, right now, to pay for such a town hall to call that mass meeting in."

He listened again. There was somebody in the next room. Murderers with the insolence the Marlow gang had shown certainly shouldn't be too cautious to kill a man in Will Marlow's office for ten thousand dollars in cash.

Will Marlow said blandly, "I'll make a deal with you, Marshal. You put that ten thousand up at the bank to be delivered to me when I've turned over a deed for a building suitable for a town hall. I'll get you a building. A sound, legal title to it, too."

Blayde drew a quick, angry breath.

"I'll take that bargain," he said harshly. "But—there's somebody in the office behind this. The men who were going to kill the man from Dos Almas went out here by the back and shot him down from ambush. I'd like to know if they've come back and are in that back room now!"

Marlow changed color, a little.

"Now, Marshal, if there's anybody in back there, I don't know a thing about it."

"They won't get out the back this time," snapped Blayde. He was bluffing, but he lusted for the killing he had come all the way from Georgia to do. "I've got a deputy out there to shoot down anybody who tries to duck. And—"

His right hand stayed ready by his holster. With his left he snatched up and flung a light bent-wood chair. It crashed into the door, then slightly ajar. The impact knocked the door wide.

Instantly there was a fusillade from within. And then a leaping figure appeared in the doorway, shooting, and Blayde's left arm jerked oddly. But he fired, his nostrils distended, and he was filled with a feeling of such gratified hatred as it made him sick to remember afterward. There was a crash of glass and he darted forward and fired through the still open door, and whirled upon Will Marlow.

Blood poured down Marlow's cheek as he sat still in his chair. He gasped unspeakable profanity. Then he saw the man at whom Blayde had fired. Will Marlow's voice broke off with a clicking sound in his throat. There was a pause, and Marlow whimpered a little, as if stunned.

"That's Cullen!" he said in a thin voice. "You killed him!"

"Well?" said Blayde, without mercy. "Was the man with him Bryant?"

"No. It was a Mex—" Will Marlow stared down at the body of his brother on the floor. He shivered. After a moment he reached up his hand and wiped at his cheek. He whimpered again. "I—I didn't know anybody was there."

Blayde went to the front window. Once he saw Will Marlow's eyes shift. He raised the muzzle of his pistol. Marlow licked his lips and was still. Blayde called coldly through the window.

Men came across the street and up the stairs. Uneasy, uncomfortable men, whose eyes nevertheless gleamed a little when they saw the dead man on the floor. Judge Harper said irritably:

"Marshal, we need law and order, not killings. How did this happen?"

"He came through the door shooting," said Blayde quietly.

"The evidence!" snapped the Judge. "What's the evidence?"

"His gun is empty," said Blayde sardonically. "He shot it empty, and a bullet nicked his brother's cheek. I fired one shot, and it should have got him in the heart. How many times would he shoot after I killed him?"

He offered one of his weapons. Judge Harper looked at it and pursed his lips. He bent and examined Cullen Marlow's emptied weapon.

"No jury'd convict you," he said peevishly. "No question about it. He shot first. No use having a trial for nothing. But Marshal Weatherby, I warn you, this is not the wild West!"

Blayde put his pistol back in its holster. He turned and went out of the office in which he had tried so hard—and partly succeeded—for the provocation of an attack upon himself. But he was not satisfied. Only one had fired at him. He'd killed only one.

At the street level he remembered the man who'd jumped out of the window. He went hungrily around to the back of the building. There was some broken glass there, and the deep imprint of a rider's high boot heels in soft earth, and the marks where a man's body had tumbled beside them. But whoever had jumped from the window in panic had got away.

Weatherby appeared.

"Come on," he said hurriedly. "Let's get back to the hacienda. I untied Yank and brought him across for you."

Blayde nodded. He went to the front of the building. Yank and Weatherby's horse waited. Blayde mounted, using only his right hand to swing into the saddle. Weatherby mounted quickly and they started off. Men all along the street stared at the two of them as they rode briskly out of town.

They had barely passed the first clump of trees beyond it when Weatherby fished a big silk kerchief out of his pocket.

"Do you need a tourniquet?" he asked jerkily. "I saw you'd put your hand in your pocket. I guessed you didn't want them to know. But if it's bleeding—"

Blayde drew his left hand out into sight.

"I'm far from crippled," he said, "but the infernal thing does hurt. It'll hurt more when the shock wears off."

He held out the arm for Weatherby to bandage it. Weatherby did a fairly expert job. When it was over he said with sudden shame:

"And I wasn't with you! I feel more and more useless all the time!"

Blayde fixed a sling to hold the hand up high.

"You were obeying orders, and you're noticing things, anyhow. You saw that I was hit. You're improving!"

He rode on. But as he seemed to think things over, his face grew darker and more bitter.

"I guess I'm a fool," he said after a little. "They're plain murderers. I could have killed Will Marlow too, before anyone came up the stairs, only I couldn't make him try to kill me! And I had to taunt Cullen into coming for me before I killed him. Why do I have to be such a fool?"

Weatherby rode beside him. The horses made their way toward the Hacienda del Norte.

"I think Antonia would say," he suggested presently, "that it was because you couldn't be a murderer yourself, Blayde."

Then Blayde turned raging eyes upon him.

"But suppose it was Bryant that was the other man in that back room?" he cried furiously. "Suppose I had all three of them there at once, and I only killed one and missed another and let the third one live? My God, if I missed Bryant, who killed my sister—"

His expression was so filled with tormenting doubts that Weatherby did not quite dare to speak again all the rest of the way back. But presently there was the sprawling, fortified place that was the home of Antonia Robles, the Hacienda del Norte.

The wound was minor, but very painful. Blayde would have gone to the huge room assigned to them and had Weatherby make a permanent job of the bandaging, but Antonia saw the silk kerchief, in places stained an ugly red, even though Blayde had put away the sling and tried to keep it out of sight.

She imperiously demanded to see. Weatherby, grinning a little bit anxiously and a little bit proudly, backed her. In the end it was Antonia who did what might be called the surgery. There was no bone broken and no important blood vessel severed. Blayde said irritably:

"It's nothing to worry about. But it's bad tactics to let

the enemy know you took a loss in any fight. That's all."

As Antonia was wrapping the last of the bandage, her brother came in. Antonia said:

"Martin fought the Marlows today, Luis. He killed one, in Will Marlow's office."

Luis said sardonically, "How many were there?"

Weatherby said, "Cullen and Will Marlow. Bryant wasn't there. Judge Harper was stamping around and swearing about"—he hesitated—"my brother acting like this was the wild West instead of a quiet, peaceful place."

"And one of the Marlows ran away?" asked Luis.

His expression was filled with a stifled anger. When he looked at Blayde, thinking him a Weatherby of Boston, he thought of the lost war, and of the wound that would make him limp clumsily all the rest of his life.

"I left Will Marlow in his office," said Blayde, "looking at the body of his brother. I have an idea that he and Bryant will really try to do something about that."

"So you rode back here," said Luis. "Most discreet!"

"If you'd like to know," said Blayde, "I was afraid."

Luis stared. To admit that one was afraid was unthinkable to him. He looked at Blayde almost with incredulity.

"I was afraid," said Blayde gently, "that I'd get killed before I got Bryant. I don't want that to happen."

"Let us trust," said Luis with excessive politeness, "that it will not."

He went out of the room, limping. Blayde frowned after him.

"Confound him! I could like that son-of-a-gun, but he keeps making me mad!"

Weatherby said ruefully, "It's because you are me, Blayde. For a Yankee to marry his sister galls him."

Antonia smiled and frowned at once. She said to Blayde:

"Martin is not discreet. He should not say such things aloud until—later. But he had told me much of you. Martin is very fortunate to have you for his friend, señor."

"You should not say such things aloud," grunted Blayde, "until—later. But it worries me that when your father hears the facts he is going to be angry. He may even think less well of"—he grimaced—"Daniel. Incidentally, you want to fuss with him, Antonia. He's a firebrand. He's got too much nerve for his own good. Anybody who's as bad a shot as he is ought to sit quiet and walk small."

Antonia looked warmly at Weatherby.

"I will scold him," she said to Blayde. "What else should I do? I will drive him—oh, terribly!—at any task you set him."

Blayde grinned at the two of them. He felt vastly older and wiser and therefore more unhappy than the two young folk. But Weatherby was very little younger than himself, if any at all, and Antonia was no more than a year younger still.

"Oh, make him learn to hit something when he shoots," he said. "If you can do that, you're a better man than I am!"

He continued to grin as they went out together. But when they were gone the grin vanished. His face grew somber.

He paced up and down the great room for a time after that. Presently he heard a shot. He went to a window. Weatherby had kicked a tin can to the base of the adobe outer wall. As Antonia watched, he fired painstakingly at it. He was bad. He was very bad. Antonia laughed and suddenly exclaimed. She ran into the house. She was out in a moment with the hat Weatherby had worn that day. It was Wild Bill Hickok's hat. She jammed it on Weatherby's head, laughing at him. She gestured at the tin can and laughed again. Weatherby made an exuberant gesture in his turn. They were completely lighthearted.

I'm getting to act like an old man, thought Blayde sourly, comparing himself with them. Old and cranky and crabbed.

He drew his pistol. As Weatherby, down below him,

aimed at the tin can, Blayde saw him conscientiously doing very nearly everything Blayde had tried hard to teach him to avoid. Blayde could tell the exact fraction of a second when the pistol would explode.

The two shots sounded as one. To Weatherby, Blayde's shot must have seemed an echo from the wall. The tin can leaped, and Weatherby fairly gaped at it. Antonia laughed with delight.

Another shot. Again Blayde fired with Weatherby. His feeling of gloom was absurdly diminished in the act of playing a practical joke on a man he honestly liked.

Weatherby tossed the tin can high. He fired at it. It leaped. He fired again, and it leaped a second time. Then Antonia saw Blayde in the act of hitting the target Weatherby fired at. She stared in astonishment at Blayde in the window, while Weatherby took off Wild Bill Hickok's hat and stared at it in amazement. Then Antonia almost choked upon her laughter. Blayde grinned at her and put his finger to his lips. She nodded confidentially and went to Weatherby.

Blayde turned, still grinning a little, from the window. And Don Felipe Robles was standing only a few feet away.

"A jest upon your brother," he said, smiling.

"He can't shoot," said Blayde apologetically, "but I like him just the same."

Don Felipe linked his arm in Blayde's.

"Don Martin," he said, "I like your brother. He is not truly a black sheep, is he?"

"That was a joke too, sir," said Blayde. "He's as good as they come, sir."

Don Felipe nodded, his eyes friendly.

"He has said the same of you, and he meant it. It is good to see brothers who are not only loyal, but who truly like each other. I congratulate your parents. But I have business to speak of, Don Martin. Mr. Will Marlow—"

Blayde's face grew hopeful. "You've just come from town? And he sends a warning that I am about to die?"

Don Felipe laughed scornfully. "Nothing so natural! No. He asked me to ask that you put into the bank the money you offered for a town-hall building for Dallas. I said at once that, since you are to be my son-in-law, I would post it immediately on your behalf. I have done so. I hope I did not offend you? It is a proper thought, that citizens should have a building in which to meet to discuss the problems of their town."

Blayde hesitated. "Of course I can only be grateful," he said wryly. "But why did Marlow make that move?"

"He said also that he cannot blame you for the death of his brother, who was a black sheep and has been a source of great grief to him."

"There's a lie in that somewhere," grunted Blayde. "That's not right. He never grieved over any killings they did!"

"Judge Harper, also," said Don Felipe dryly, "observed to me that if things continue as they have begun, Dallas will become as it should be, a law-abiding, peaceful, Eastern town."

Blayde grinned. "With no wild-West aspect at all. How many people were killed in Dallas before I came?"

Don Felipe reflected. "In Dallas itself, two—in the month before today. In the county I think five in the same time. That is much too many, of course."

"There were three killings in Dallas this morning," Blayde pointed out. "I only did one of them, but still—"

"Don Martin," said Antonia's father, "when you wish to take the field against the Marlows with a posse behind you, I offer my *vaqueros*, my son, and myself."

Blayde said ruefully, "Judge Harper insists that I have to use the citizens of the town of Dallas. He insists that they need to do it."

"My men also," said Don Felipe firmly. "Some of them speak English badly, and a few not at all. So it is especially necessary that they ride in a posse and feel the obligations and the privileges of citizens. You see?"

"I do." Blayde added, "They'd be especially good fighting men, with the training Don Luis has given them."

"So I believe," said Don Felipe sedately. "Now I would like to speak to you of serious matters. Will you come into the library?"

He ushered Blayde into the huge paneled room with its walls of bookcases filled. There were modern books, to be sure, but more impressive were the shelves of ancient, hand-written volumes. Some were hand-written because printing had not yet been invented at the time they were written, and some later ones were hand-written because governments watched all printed matter closely for signs of aspirations to freedom. Don Felipe offered Blayde a chair, and placed a box of cheroots at his elbow.

"Now, as one man to another," he began politely, "there is business to be done. It should begin with the establishment of identities. . . ."

A full two hours later, Blayde and Don Felipe came out of the library together. Blayde went in search of Weatherby. He found him alone in the big room they shared.

"Martin," said Blayde, "this business can't go on."

Weatherby jerked his head around.

"I mean it," said Blayde. "I just had a long talk with Don Felipe. He believes me you, of course. The talk began very formally. He said that it should begin with the establishment of identities—and then he said it would be absurd to go into such a matter. I felt like a scoundrel. Then he talked business as one would to a son-in-law. It should not have happened. You've got to take back your identity in this house, anyhow."

Weatherby looked a little bit sick at heart.

"Things aren't as simple in any way as I thought they'd be," he said slowly. "I'm beginning to feel that a fool like myself doesn't belong here. Just now I tried to shoot at a target. You suggested it jokingly to Antonia. But I tried it. I missed everything, every time. Then Antonia told me to try on Wild Bill's hat. She ran and got it. I did."

"I couldn't resist it," said Blayde remorsefully. "Of course, I didn't think of it until—"

"I know." Weatherby nodded quite seriously. "The thing is, Blayde, that it fooled me. I actually thought, until Antonia laughed at me, that wearing Wild Bill Hickok's hat had somehow, inexplicably, made it possible for me to shoot straight. Silly, wasn't it?"

"I'm sorry," said Blayde. "It was a chance to play a joke, and I couldn't resist it."

"I know," said Weatherby again, unsmiling. "No malice. I think you like me well enough, Blayde. But it made me realize that I'm pretty much of a fool."

"Contradiction in terms there," observed Blayde. "You can't be really a fool unless you're sure you aren't."

"Maybe I'm outgrowing it," said Weatherby. "Maybe. But Blayde—God knows Antonia is the most wonderful girl who ever lived. Do you think that—that such a fool as I am worthy of her?"

Blayde went over to the window. He looked out.

"The only test of a man's worthiness for a particular woman," he said, "is the way she feels about it. If she feels that he is, there's no other test. It wouldn't be very good for her to marry a man who was worthy of her in other people's eyes if she happened not to like him."

Weatherby thought it over.

"There's that," he agreed. "Yes. I don't suppose any man is really worthy of any woman, is he?"

"It's at least an appropriate frame of mind for an engaged man," said Blayde. "Hold to it."

"I'd like," said Weatherby painfully, "to feel that Antonia wasn't making too bad a choice in marrying me. I care that much about her, you see."

Blayde nodded. "One would feel that way."

"How do you know?" Weatherby lifted his head again. "You said you'd had no romantic experience." When Blayde did not answer, he said in a queer voice, "Blayde! She's wonderful, and you know it. But don't tell me that you—"

He stood up, suddenly pale. Blayde put his hand on Weatherby's shoulder.

"I've been talking to Don Felipe. About the future

of Dallas County. About railroads, and cotton, and how
the damage the war has done everywhere has to be re-
paired by men working harder than ever before, and
thinking straighter, and forgetting everything that happened yesterday, and planning confidently for what is
to happen tomorrow. You should have had that talk,
Martin. If you'll stop searching your soul for flaws in
your own character, and start thinking about the work
that's got to be done here after I go away, you'll feel
better and do better, too."

There was a little rattling clamor outside. A horseman
had arrived at the gate of the ranch, and was riding into
the courtyard within it.

"I have been bothered, Blayde," admitted Weatherby.
"I— It was very silly of me, thinking I was in love with
Antonia up in Boston. Since I've been here, compared to
the way I feel about her now, it was—practically child-
ish. I really know what it's like to care for someone now.
And it irritates me that I have to pretend to be only
your brother—though it was my idea."

"We can end it," said Blayde. "After all, my job's a
third done."

Weatherby looked obstinate. "It serves me right. I
started it this way. We'll finish it this way."

There was a respectful knock on the door. Blayde
opened it. A swarthy servant stood there.

"Don Felipe asks that you come to him, señores."

Blayde nodded. The servant disappeared.

"One thing is good," Blayde told Weatherby. "Don
Felipe does like you. For yourself. When I've gone, and
the reason for the masquerade has been told him, he'll
still like you."

Weatherby shook his head. "But I'm not so sure that
I like myself. Let's go see what's happened."

Don Felipe was waiting in the great hall. His face
was dark with anger.

"Within the hour," he said coldly, "there has been
another killing in Dallas. Your actions of this morning,
Don Martin, aroused hope among the citizens. There

was talk of gathering under your leadership to put down
crime. Mr. Walters, of the Chuckaway, posted a sheet
of paper in his establishment for persons daring to volunteer to serve in a posse under you to sign. He signed
it first himself."

Blayde waited. Weatherby said:

"Well?"

"The buckshot that killed him," said Don Felipe icily,
"destroyed the paper also. It is spattered with his blood.
It is said that Bryant Marlow killed Mr. Walters."

Weatherby swore under his breath, his hands clenched.
Blayde said:

"I think there must be something more."

"There is. I placed ten thousand dollars at the bank,"
said Don Felipe with the same formidable chill in his
voice. "It was to be paid when Mr. Will Marlow or anyone else offered a deed to a building suitable for a town
hall for Dallas. I have just had a message from Marlow.
He tells me that he believes the building formerly owned
by Mr. Walters will serve as a town hall, and he assures
me he will have purchased it from Mr. Walters' widow
by tomorrow. In effect, he tells me that he has had a
murder committed to meet my wishes, and dares me to
do anything about it!"

"Still," said Blayde doggedly, "he will have to wait
his turn. I don't mean to risk losing Bryant for anything
or anybody!"

Chapter Nine

UNDOUBTEDLY, at this same time but in a different place, some young Eskimo dwelled sentimentally upon the charms of a maiden who could chew sealskin into the material for boots more perfectly than any other damsel of his tribe. There was undoubtedly a youthful Chilean who reflected upon the impenetrable bars that guarded his sweetheart from his fascination. A German peasant youth doubtless meditated upon his Gretchen's buxom charm. And in far-off Borneo, a proud young warrior carrying home the head of a stranger he had potted from behind a bush would be thinking how a Borneo maiden's eyes would shine when he showed his gamy trophy to her father.

All of them, doubtless, were wholly normal in their separate ways. The way of a man with a maiden's image in his heart is different in different places, but only in minor items. Weatherby had talked to Blayde of his own unworthiness, and had felt a stab of imagined jealousy. And then he hunted up Antonia and very contentedly looked at her with great tenderness while she played on a vast square rosewood piano that had traveled eight weeks by oxcart from the ship that had landed it in Mexico two generations previously.

Antonia said softly, "But Martin . . . who is he?"

"An outlaw," said Weatherby.

The notes of the piano paused, and went on again in a trivial, abstracted fashion.

"Why? Did he—kill someone?"

"His family was killed," said Weatherby. "His mother and father and sister. By the Marlows. In Georgia. He has trailed them all the way here."

Antonia played abstractedly with one hand only. Blayde sat silently in a chair on the far side of the great hall of the hacienda. There was a book beside him, but he had put it down. He smoked moodily. Antonia's father was highly modern in his views. He saw no real reason why Antonia should not talk with her fiancé—whom he like enormously—so long as they sat in a well-lighted room with the doors open, with servants passing from time to time, so long as Antonia played the piano, and so long as someone else was with them. Obviously, he considered that Blayde was her fiancé. But Blayde sat alone and Weatherby leaned over the piano in a romantic attitude.

Antonia said, "Had he no wife or sweetheart, that he devoted his life to revenge?"

"He did not," said Weatherby. "And it isn't revenge. It's justice."

Antonia raised her eyes to him, and dropped them again.

"Is it a blow to you to know?" Weatherby asked anxiously.

"He is your friend," said Antonia. "If you trust him, so should I."

She struck a few more notes while Weatherby swelled a little.

"And—he killed someone today," she said.

"Who badly needed it."

Antonia's fingers strayed over the keys.

"Has he ever killed anyone else?"

"Perhaps in the war," said Weatherby. "One can't tell. I may have killed somebody at Antietam. I fired at them. Whether I hit them or not I don't know. I might have— by accident."

He smiled ruefully. But she said gravely:

"I hope it was not your bullet that struck Luis. He is very bitter. But has your friend killed anyone besides this man today?"

"There were two or three men in Missouri," he said awkwardly. "The Marlows had sent them to kill him. One of them, anyhow. They intended to kill him in the middle of a crowd at a horse race. He shot his way out. He is hard to kill."

Then he remembered the poster Blayde had put up everywhere, offering five thousand dollars' reward for information about the Marlows, and how it often showed up beside the Federal circulars demanding his arrest. He told Antonia, thinking it would amuse her.

"I collected the five thousand reward," he added, humorously, "because I happened to know where they were. He paid it to me."

Antonia looked at him inscrutably. She struck chords with her left hand.

"Did he ever kill anyone else?"

"On the way down," admitted Weatherby with some reluctance, "we came on a town that was being raided. . . ."

He told her about the town of Callao. He told it honestly, wryly picturing himself as standing guard over the town marshal and his deputy while Blayde went into the town and began the cleaning-up process, of which he did the largest part. Antonia went a little pale.

"I suppose it shocks you," said Weatherby uncomfortably, "but he's no murderer, Antonia. Every man he's ever killed has been armed and trying to kill him. And not one was in a personal quarrel. They were not duels. Each time he was defending something he believed in."

Antonia determinedly began to play an actual musical composition. It had a great many trills and grace notes, such as a well-brought-up girl would naturally learn to play in the process of becoming an accomplished young lady.

Suddenly she stopped and said, "What did you do with the five thousand dollars he paid you, Martin?"

"I'm really the United States marshal, you know," said Weatherby awkwardly, "and it was really government property. So I returned it to the government, with a full explanation. I made a very careful report to the attorney general. I wrote to my family, too, telling them everything. I asked them—"

He lowered his voice. She bent her head close to listen, abstractedly striking notes from time to time. Blayde shifted in his chair. His eyes went toward the piano. He saw Antonia bending toward Weatherby, her dark hair close to him, while he spoke softly. It was a pose that was romance itself.

Weatherby finished what he was saying. And Antonia ceased even to pretend to play. She looked at him and said warmly:

"Sometimes, Martinito, I have wondered why I thought you would be a person I could love. I do not wonder now!"

Weatherby flushed. He said, "Hush! But you will not tell him! Not until I hear—"

"I am proud," said Antonia, "that I am to marry you, Martin."

The silence and the emphasis with which she said it carried the words to Blayde. His expression did not change. But he got leisurely to his feet and strolled to the tall, floor-length window. They did not notice. After a little, he stepped out.

It was very beautiful out of doors. This was early in the night, and an almost full moon already rode high, and the stars seemed very bright and near. There was that curious pleasant smell that hot sunshine leaves in the air even after night has fallen and the coolness has come, besides the smell of the range outside and the flowers of Antonia's garden. Somewhere, where the *vaqueros* lived, a guitar made singing noises and a man's voice came unself-consciously through the night in a love song.

Blayde moved restlessly. On such a night as this, one could kill an enemy with extra zest, or make love with additional ardor. Neither was quite a practical pursuit for Blayde at the moment. He had contrived a plan that might enable him to fulfill all the purpose of his journeying since the surrender, and at the same time succeed in carrying out the genuinely desirable purpose of Judge Harper. It was desirable that the citizens of Dallas should take over their own defense. The idea was approved by Don Felipe. It would take time to come to fruition. Per-

haps twenty-four hours. Meanwhile he had opportunity
neither for a killing nor for romance, and he was restless.

Someone challenged, by the gate. A voice answered.
It was Don Luis, Antonia's brother. He rode in. Blayde
strolled toward the stables. The horseman rode toward
them also. He dismounted and said sharply:

"Quién es?"

"Good evening, Don Luis," said Blayde. "It is too pleasant a night to stay indoors. I think I shall saddle up and
go for a ride."

There was a pause. Then Luis said quietly:

"My horse is fresh enough. And I think that yours
needed a new shoe, and that one has to be made because
of its large size. I would be pleased if you rode my horse,
Don—Martin."

Blayde was amazed, but he said, "Thank you. Of
course."

Luis Robles said in a queer tone, "I went to Dallas
to make the arrangements you discussed with my father.
Mrs. Walters—she whose husband was killed today—will
do as you suggest."

"It was Bryant Marlow who killed him?" asked Blayde.

"There seems to be no doubt," Luis told him. Then he
paused. "I also spoke with Señor Coulter. He tells me
that my prejudice against you is unjustified. I have been
discourteous to you. I wish to express my regret."

He offered his hand. Blayde took it. He was puzzled
and a trifle uncomfortable.

"I'm afraid," Blayde said awkwardly, "that anyone
riding in as I did would be—unattractive to Antonia's
brother."

Luis Robles did not answer. Blayde said again:

"Bryant Marlow did the killing. Does anybody know
where he is now?"

"No. He keeps out of sight. I think there must be some
plan. I suggest that you take care. But my horse has the
eyes of a cat."

"And I," said Blayde, "will practice the caution of a
mouse. Thank you, Don Luis."

He swung up into the saddle. This horse was a mare and a smaller animal than Yank, but she tossed her head and went willingly enough toward the courtyard gate.

Weatherby came out of the house, having missed Blayde. He called. Blayde answered, reining in the mare to wait for him.

"Where are you going?" asked Weatherby. He added under his breath as Luis Robles moved away, "Look, Antonia and I can't very well talk when you aren't around!"

Blayde said with careful detachment, "It makes me uncomfortable to be around while you talk. I've stayed quiet ever since this morning. I want some fresh air."

"You're wounded!" objected Weatherby. "You should not go riding alone."

Blayde did not bother to answer that. He reined the mare around again toward the gate.

"And you can't arrest Bryant Marlow by yourself!" insisted Weatherby anxiously.

"Even if I knew where he was," said Blayde curtly, "I wouldn't try to—arrest him."

The *vaquero* by the gate challenged again. A woman's voice answered. It seemed overwrought and strained. It spoke English.

Without a word, Blayde moved quickly to the gate. Weatherby came with him, on foot. There was a horse outside the gate, in the moonlight. It pawed nervously. Its rider was a woman. She said stridently:

"I tell you, I want to talk to Marshal Weatherby. You go git him!"

Blayde said, "I'm Marshal Weatherby, ma'am. Who are you?"

"I'm Mrs. Walters. Mrs. Bill Walters. My Bill got killed today."

"Yes," said Blayde.

Weatherby was close beside his stirrup. Blayde tapped him significantly on the shoulder and added, "What's the trouble, ma'am?"

"Bryant Marlow's the trouble, Marshal! Bullyin' an' threatenin' for his brother Will! He's bringin' a bill of

sale tonight, all made out for me to sign over all of
Bill's leavin's."

She seemed to sob. The moonlight did not lend
glamour to her appearance. Her hair was blonde and
stringy. She held herself defiantly even as she sobbed.
Blayde's face, as Weatherby saw it in the moonlight, was
curiously flinty of expression.

"Where's he going to bring the bill of sale?"

"To my house. Right outside of Dallas. Can you—can
you do something to protect me, Marshal?"

Blayde laughed a little.

"It'll be a pleasure, ma'am. I'll come with you right
now!"

"But you can't go alone!" protested Weatherby
fiercely.

"I can and will," said Blayde softly. "But you can do
me a favor, my friend. Go and tell Don Luis that Mrs.
Walters came to the gate and that I've gone with her
to guard her against Bryant Marlow. To her house just
outside of Dallas. Understand? Tell him every word of
that—Daniel!"

Again his hand tapped Weatherby's shoulder commandingly. And Weatherby was confused. He watched
uneasily as Blayde rode out of the gate and said:

"Lead the way, ma'am!"

The woman reined about and started off at top speed.
Blayde let out the mare to follow her. The two running
mounts dwindled to mere blurs upon the moonlit range.

Weatherby stared after them, which was unfortunate,
because it cost time. It was long minutes before he gave
Antonia's brother the message. And then he was
astounded when that young man, stiff leg and all, leaped
up and swore furiously, and then began to shout angry
orders in sibilant Spanish. He saw Weatherby's expression and snapped:

"That was not Mrs. Walters! I left her in Dallas an
hour ago! It was a trap! A decoy! It was a woman come
to lead him into an ambush the Marlows have set! And
he knew it!"

He went raging out of the house, and already there were the men he had trained, piling onto wiry horses in readiness to follow him anywhere. They went out of the gateway in a hurtling mass of horseflesh and vanished in the night.

Weatherby went forlornly back into the house. Antonia's father was crisply giving orders for special vigilance at the sentry posts, for the closing of the outer gate, and for such measures as could be taken to make the ranch safe in the absence of most of its defenders.

But Blayde went on, away from the house. The moonlight was like molten silver poured on the foliage of the range. The woman kept on hard ahead, so fast that it was not easy to ask her questions. It was a curious ride to be taking, and a curious sensation as he rode. But there was an unholy exultation in it, too. On such nights as this dogs howl dismally at the moon. On such nights human lovers murmur nonsense that they themselves cannot remember from one moment to the next. And on such nights it is very, very easy to be wrought up to frenzied deeds.

Blayde knew that his sister had been killed at night, by a campfire of bushwhackers led by the three Marlows, when she managed to snatch a revolver and open fire with it. When he thought of that happening, it was never easy for him to be calm. But to think of it at night, and on such a night as this, while riding to an ambush made ready for him by her murderers . . .

Blayde's teeth showed white in the moon shadow his hat brim cast upon his face.

They rode fast. When Blayde would have overtaken her, the woman bent over her horse's neck and rode faster.

Then Blayde suddenly reined aside. The woman rode on. He waited. Don Luis' mare took long, deep breaths, comfortable and soothing. There was a small clump of two or three trees that concealed man and horse together. There was a long stillness. Then the woman's voice.

"Marshal Weatherby . . . Marshal Weatherby . . ."

Blayde continued to wait. Minutes later the woman reappeared, straining her eyes through the moonlight, looking for him. She rode into the shadow of the trees.

"Where's Bryant?" asked Blayde pleasantly, almost at her side.

She started, and her horse danced away.

"You scared me, Marshal!"

"Where's Bryant? He's your sweetheart, isn't he?"

"Marshal!" she protested shrilly. "You ain't goin' to insult me like that, and my Bill not hardly cold—"

"I had a message from Mrs. Walters," said Blayde very quietly, "not ten minutes before you came pretending to be her. You're supposed to lead me into an ambush. I'm supposed to be killed by Bryant." He paused. "I shan't kill you. Where's Bryant?"

"I was never so insulted in my life!"

"Stop it!" said Blayde with a dangerous coldness. "What do you get out of this, anyhow? Did Bryant Marlow ever keep a single promise he ever made you? What did he promise you for bringing me to him to be killed? No," he repeatedly angrily, "I'm not going to kill you. But what did he and Will Marlow promise you?" Then he said roughly, "Who are you, anyhow?"

She stared at him in the moonlight. Then she put one hand on her hip, cockily.

"If you want to know, Mr. Marshal Weatherby, they promised me plenty. And Bryant never kep' a promise to me yet, an' he never will because he's a snake an' other things, an' what are you goin' to do about it? Make me some promises too?"

"Who are you?" he demanded again.

"Me? I'm Flo," she said stridently. "You can call me Bryant's wife—and better'n he deserves!"

"He lets you take a chance for him," said Blayde grimly. "Lets you risk your life in an ambush where his gang is going to shoot me down. And if he happens to be tired of you, it'd be natural enough for you to get a bullet at the same time!"

"You know a lot, you do!" she cried furiously. "What do you know about Bryant an' me?"

"I know," said Blayde, "that if I shot you dead and left you here—no matter what I did to you—Bryant wouldn't care. And you know it too. So you're going to go back to him, and he'll swear at you for not bringing me. And you'll know that if you had brought me you'd get no thanks, and if I'd killed you it wouldn't have bothered him a bit. You don't matter a snap of his fingers to him! If he finds a younger or a prettier girl he'll kick you out, unless you know too much about him for him to let you go, and then he'll kill you. He's lied to you every minute he's known you when it would do any good, and when he has nothing to gain by it he doesn't bother to lie. You figured luring me to him would make him think something of you again. You know it wouldn't, but you tried it anyhow. And now you'll go back to him without me, and he'll curse you for a useless fool, and if I'd killed you he wouldn't care!"

It was partly the moonlight that made him savage; the moonlight and its urge to frenzied action and speech and sensation. But a part of it was deliberate. A man who has led a regiment in wartime may know very little about the sort of romance that a well-brought-up young man and a carefully raised young girl consider normal and thrilling and remarkable, but Blayde knew the kind of hysterical squabbling that would take place in a bushwhacker's camp when there was a woman who followed a special man. There had been cases in his own regiment.

The woman suddenly cursed him shrilly.

"What're you tryin' to do?" she cried. "Don't I know all that?"

"I'm trying to hurt you," said Blayde savagely. "You know you hate him anyway. If you realize that he makes you hate yourself, you'll quit him—and miss what's coming to him!"

She glared at him. Suddenly she spat, and whirled her horse, and dug her heels into its sides. The horse went plunging away into the darkness.

Blayde watched, his eyes burning. She was going back to Bryant Marlow. If he rode with her, he would ride into a prepared ambush. If he trailed her . . .

From where he sat watching, the line of her riding was directly under the stars of the Little Bear. He sat quietly for a while, listening to the retreating footsteps of her horse. He listened also for the sounds that might be Don Luis coming with the *vaqueros* of the Hacienda del Norte to take care of the ambuscade Blayde had sent word of. He had no doubt that Don Luis would follow as soon as Weatherby gave the message.

But Don Luis and his cavalcade did not appear. Actually, they were spread out and listening tensely for the sounds of hoofbeats by which they might follow Blayde and the woman. But they could not know the woman's haste. They had raced headlong, and thought they had gone on past the pair. But in fact they were still well behind.

Blayde could wait only so long, or he would have no trail to follow. The line of the woman's flight would be good for a short time only after she reached the useless trap.

He gave her time to get well ahead. Then he rode a quarter mile to the eastward and set out on a parallel line for the point on the horizon that would be just under the Little Bear.

He was in that trembling, urgent mood which is so close to berserk fury, and which can, without warning, change to impassioned tenderness. His eyes were unnaturally bright, and his ears were unnaturally keen, and the muscles of his body seemed somehow much more tuned up to any imaginable demand than was anywhere near normal. One part of his mind thought with proper, detached precision. The other was filled with confused images. He saw Antonia, and he saw Weatherby, and he saw the mistily remembered pictures of his parents and sister, and the vividly imagined pictures of their murders. But over and over again he saw Antonia at the piano as she had been only half an hour since, with

Weatherby bending over to say something very quietly in her ear.

He thought cynically to himself, The trouble with me is that I'm jealous. That was drearily amusing. He had no right to be jealous. He was an outlaw. Officially, he was even a dead man. He was an impostor, pretending to be an officer of the government that would shoot or hang him if it ever laid hands upon him. He had no name, no possessions—he even rode a borrowed horse at the moment—and the only thing he actually owned was a blood feud with two surviving murderers. He had surely no right to be jealous of anybody or anything.

He thrust those thoughts away. He told himself deliberately that even if he did not find Bryant tonight, any man who had joined Bryant to ambush and murder him would be a man who had done murder or worse as part of the Marlow brothers' reconstituted gang. Any man who followed Bryant tonight could justly pay for what some other man who had followed him in Georgia had done. And there might be half a dozen or more. . . .

Two miles, and he dismounted to listen. Four, and he heard distant hoofbeats on the earth. He rode on ahead, filled with this strange mood that was so horribly consistent with the moonlight. Little timber patches were pools of utter darkness. Clear spaces were pools and lakes of silver-white light upon the earth.

Presently he was ahead and waiting, where thick timber on two sides made it certain that the hoofbeats he could hear would come this way. He heard the thrashing of brush as horses forced their way through belly-high growth. He heard voices, muttering sulkily.

His own mare nickered in friendly fashion.

Blayde ground his teeth. Then he roughened his voice.

"Bry-ant . . ." he called through cupped hands. "Got a message from Will!"

The approaching horses came on. A snarling voice said:

"A'right. Heah we are."

"I'm comin'," said Blayde.

He rode forward boldly. The thrashings were closer,
ahead. He saw dim shapes in the moonlit brushwood.
Then a woman's voice screamed:

"Bryant! That's him! The Marshal!"

Blayde charged furiously.

In the mood he was in, compounded of hatred and
jealousy and grief and a terrible loneliness, that charge
was the most satisfying action he could have found.

There were dark trees looming on either side, and a
wide avenue of stars overhead, but the moon was hidden
here, and the brushwood was an erratic pattern of vague
and yielding forms in which eight mounted figures were
vaguely placed. But a gun flash at the right gave him
a target. Don Luis' mare put back her ears and flashed
ahead. There was a moment's crazy confusion. His own
pistols thundered. There were rearing mounts all about
him, and weapons exploding luridly, and cries and
thrashings and figures flinging themselves out of his way.
Then he was through.

He was fifty yards away before the mare stopped her
headlong rush. He wheeled her about to plunge back,
but he heard Bryant Marlow's bellowed commands:

"Off them hawsses! Rifles out! Git him eff'n he comes
back!"

That was sound military strategy. No cavalry charge
can be pushed home against rapid aimed fire from a
larger number of dismounted men. Blayde, charging
alone even in semiblackness, would be bound to be
limned against the sky for dismounted men in the brushwood to bring down.

His teeth showed momentarily. He wheeled the mare
again, made her reins secure against trailing, and slipped
off her back as he slapped her flank with a pistol barrel.
She fled at a dead run, and Blayde remained on foot to
turn exactly the bushwhacker's tactic against them. When
they pursued the fleeing horse, he would have them
against the sky as they neared him. It would be sheer
butchery of men who were much more accustomed to
doing the butchering themselves.

But Bryant's voice raised again:

"Ne-mind! Come on! Git goin'! He knowed we was layin' for him! He's gone to git the rest. Move now!"

Again, that was sound military reasoning on the information Bryant had. His followers fled with him through the night, leaving two of their number behind, and leaving Blayde raging and furious on foot, but not so furious that he would expose his presence to eight man who could dismount also and hunt him down at leisure in the underbrush.

It was near to dawn when he rode up to the gateway of the Hacienda del Norte. It had been a good two hours before he found the horse of one of the two dead members of the Marlow gang. It had taken him nearly an hour to capture the animal. The ride back to the hacienda was a dreary, discouraged affair. In the cold gray light before sunrise the horizon seemed incredibly far away and all things seemed without color, and he was bitter with himself for not having handled the affair more soundly, because Bryant Marlow had been within gun reach of him and had lived.

He was weary, too, because though the injury to his arm was of no great consequence, he had lost a good deal of blood. So it was a tired and dreary man upon a drooping horse that rode up to the high adobe wall and dully answered the sentry's challenge.

"*Señor*," said the *vaquero* sentry agitatedly, "you rode out upon Don Luis' horse and she came back alone! A bullet had struck her saddle!"

"Did it?" asked Blayde uninterestedly. He hadn't noticed, in the fight in the brushwood.

"Don Felipe thought you dead! He and Don Luis and Don Daniel seek you now! They sent back for old Carlos to try to trail back to you even in the moonlight! But they have no hope!"

Blayde rode in through the gateway and dismounted heavily.

"If there's anybody you can send to tell them I'm all right, you'd better do it."

He turned over the dead bandit's horse to a popeyed stable boy and went drearily into the house. He entered the great hall where the piano was. Candles burned there, beginning to fade in the pale light outside.

There was a small figure bent over a table, its head in its arms as if weeping silently. Blayde stared at it. He went over to the table. He said gently:

"Antonia."

She gasped and sprang to her feet. Her face was dead-white, and she had been weeping for a long, long time. She stared at him with wide, shocked, unbelieving eyes.

"What's the matter?" asked Blayde tiredly. "Anything happen to Martin?"

She shook her head almost absently, staring at him as if she could not believe what she saw. She moved a step toward him, and put out her hand, and touched him shakily. He was real. And with the contact, Antonia caught her breath, and her eyes filmed with tears, and she swayed as if about to fall. Blayde caught her quickly.

Then she began to weep in great gasping sobs, and all unconsciously her arms went about him and clung desperately as she wept terribly because of her joy that he was alive.

And Blayde's expression was an extraordinary mixture of bitterness with other and quite dissimilar emotions.

Chapter Ten

THE SUN came up, and smote the adobe walls outside with crimson light. It was reflected in the high windows that went from floor to ceiling of this huge paneled room. Antonia sat in a great carved chair and looked at Blayde. She was still pale, but her eyes seemed somehow to smile at him.

"You see that it's become impossible for me to marry Martin now, don't you?" she asked quietly.

"Why?"

"Because I love you," said Antonia. "I like Martin too much to marry him while I love someone else. He would not wish me to."

Blayde paced up and down. His boots were muddy. His clothing was powdered with pollen or some such stuff that the brushwood had shed upon him. His face was lined with weariness. The bandage about his left hand and arm had grown stained again. He was not a glamorous figure.

"I'm an outlaw, Antonia," he said harshly. "The United States government wants me. For stealing."

She shook her head. "No. Martin told me everything. Not stealing."

"I've killed men," he said bitterly. "I'm— It would be impossible even if it weren't dishonorable because Martin's my friend."

She smiled then, a very small smile.

"I have only to tell Martin," she said quietly, "that it is you whom I love, and he will tell my father that he loves me too much to marry me, because I love someone else."

"But," said Blayde sardonically, "it happens to be disgraceful to care about me."

"My father likes you," said Antonia, with an air of patient reasoning, "and he knows men. And my brother did not like you, and now he does, and he knows men."

Blayde shook his head. He paced up and down. Antonia tilted her head a little on one side.

"Are you about to say that you are not worthy of me, Blayde?" she asked, smiling wistfully. "Remember there is but one test of that."

Blayde said irritably, "He told you that too? Haven't you two talked of anything at all but me?"

"Now that I think," admitted Antonia, "not very much else. I—I told him that I was proud to know that he was to be my husband because—"

"What?" demanded Blayde suspiciously.

"Because he said something about you that only a very honest man would say," said Antonia. "I think that Martin would be my second choice of a husband, Blayde." Then she laughed a little, shakily. "Hear how I talk! Do you realize that I am disputing with you? That I make a most impudent proposal that you marry me, without even asking if you wish to?"

"If I wish to!" said Blayde despairingly. "But it is impossible!"

Antonia stood up. She swept him a deep curtsy.

"And it is impossible for me to marry anyone else. I shall go to my room and think of more arguments with which to press my suit for your hand."

She moved toward the door. And Weatherby had been right, beside a tiny campfire on the plains on the way down to Texas. He'd said that when Antonia crossed a room, it was the most graceful movement that could be imagined. It was. But she stopped near the door, and put out her hands, and her eyes were bright with tears.

"Please, Blayde? Please?"

He took her hands in his, and then quite without volition he drew her to him and kissed her. Then he ground his teeth and drew back.

She smiled at him and went on to the door. She turned there and said resolutely:

"I am not ashamed! I am very proud!"

Then he heard her run to her room, weeping a little.

Blayde stood still for a moment. Then he spread out his hands in a gesture of weary helplessness and went to his own room.

He was shaving when Weatherby came in. Blayde had heard the horses tramping in the gateway. He'd looked out the window and seen two limp, jerking figures brought in behind two riders. His face was lathered when Weatherby pumped his hand, wordlessly, his expression one of overwhelming relief and joy.

"We hunted everywhere, Blayde. I messed things up, as usual. I should have told Don Luis instantly what you'd told me to, but I didn't see the urgency of it." He grimaced. "I see why I stayed a private in the ranks during the war. I'm pretty stupid, Blayde. What happened?"

"Nothing much," said Blayde. He was very far from happy. He liked Weatherby. And he saw no hope whatever for himself.

"Don Felipe sent back for old Carlos, the tracker," said Weatherby. "I don't know how he did it, in the moonlight, but he led us to a place where he said you'd charged a gang and ridden through it. There were two dead men for proof. We brought them in. But somebody was wounded, and because of the light we couldn't be sure who. We thought maybe it was you. We were going to trail on, come daybreak, and either rescue you or kill somebody, when the messenger from here called us back."

Blayde said, "Yes."

He went back to his shaving. As the lather came off, his face looked pinched and somber. Weatherby sat down and pulled off his boots.

"In passing, the *vaqueros* say those dead men are notorious as horse thieves and the like. Don Felipe agreed, and said that Judge Harper would sputter indignantly and then say that as no jury would possibly convict anybody who killed them, there was no use in taking any action." Weatherby grinned. "I like Texas, Blayde. It's so different from Boston."

Blayde began to put on a shirt.

"I feel filthy," said Weatherby, "and I don't care. And it feels good to get my boots off, but I'll enjoy putting them on again to ride to Dallas. Did you know that Texas is an Indian word, Blayde? It means 'Friend.' Antonia told me."

Blayde knotted a flowing tie. "I think I've gone through all I can take, Martin. I'm going to give you back your marshal's badge and finish up what I came here for. Then I'll ride on."

"What? Where?" demanded Weatherby blankly.

"I've several destinations in mind," said Blayde curtly.

Weatherby's forehead wrinkled helplessly. Then he said, "What is your business here?"

Blayde looked at his sardonically. "The Marlows. You know it."

"I'm not sure. Why are they your business?" insisted Weatherby. He went on, "You'll say because they murdered your family. It's not that at all. If the law had taken them and punished them, would you have rescued them from jail to take your own revenge? My dear fellow, you know your business isn't revenge!"

Blayde said caustically, "It might be interesting to know just what it is!"

Weatherby said earnestly, "Just plain decency, Blayde. I'm pretty stupid, but I can see that. You didn't take me under your wing for revenge or profit. You didn't go into Callao to get even with anybody. You didn't shoot into Will Marlow's office window yesterday morning for revenge. You were keeping a man from being murdered. He was murdered later, but that didn't change what you did, or why."

"You think I'm a sort of knight-errant," said Blayde in mirthless amusement, "without fear and without reproach? I assure you I'm not!"

"I've seen no fear," said Weatherby loyally, "and I know of no reproach—"

"I do!" said Blayde angrily. "And you will!"

"It doesn't matter," insisted Weatherby. "We were on opposite sides in the war, but we fought for the same

thing—what we believed was right. That's what all of us
fight for, instead of kings. And that's what you've been
fighting for, and that's your business! One officer in
Georgia was a fool. He didn't care what bushwhackers
did, as long as they did it to Confederates. He was wrong.
You were right to go after justice. But it wasn't and it
isn't revenge!"

"A very flattering analysis," said Blayde bitterly. "I'm
an outlaw because I believe in decent things. What have
I got out of it? Believing in decency doesn't pay!"

"Do you believe for pay?" demanded Weatherby. "Do
I?"

Blayde looked at him for what seemed a long time.

"Damyankee," he said presently. "No, you don't. I
ought to hate your guts. But almost thou persuadest me
to be a Union man—if the rest were like you. But they're
not. And to keep on like this means I have to continue to
lie to Don Felipe and Don Luis, and to Antonia and
everybody else. For decency!"

"Maybe in this case," conceded Weatherby, "for friendship. Because I am the United States marshal here. I'm
letting you do the work because you're better at it than
I am. I'm hopelessly bad at it. But if you throw up the
job, I'll have to try to do it. And I may be useless, but
I think you believe I'll try."

"I'll give you that," said Blayde grudgingly. "You will
try. And get killed. So you're blackmailing me—and I
think you'll wish you hadn't."

He stalked to the great hall where Don Felipe and his
son, Don Luis, were sipping at cups of corrosively strong
coffee. He accepted a cup. He told them, at first stiffly
and then with a sort of detached humor, of his thought
that Don Luis would follow swiftly after himself and the
woman Flo, and that he'd expected to guess when they
approached the ambush by her actions, when he'd hoped
to attack the ambush with the force Don Luis would have
brought along discreetly behind him.

"Your men are trained to fight," he told Don Luis.
"I could tell that when they stopped me. The man who

led that little patrol was a well-trained noncommissioned officer. When you've got trained noncoms, you've got fighting men."

Don Luis' eyes warmed at the praise.

"Now, I've got an idea," said Blayde. He was still formidable and grim in his thoughts, but his manner showed only seriousness. "I'd like your opinion on it. It appears that Will Marlow and his brothers and their gang have been able almost to do as they pleased, with impunity, because they never allowed opposition to them to be even expressed without instant and deadly punishment. When Walters proposed that men volunteer to put down outlawry, he was immediately killed. That has happened before."

"It has always happened before," said Don Felipe. "My herds have been raided often enough, but I still have cattle because we did not have to speak of our plans to organize in their defense. Luis trained our *vaqueros,* and they are a good force. Yet they alone could not rally support about themselves, because many of them speak only Spanish."

There was definite irony in the fact, but it was a fact nevertheless.

"My thought," said Blayde, "is that you have already given old Carlos a guard of two men—he would not take more—and he is now trying to follow the trail of the gang I fought last night back to their hideout. With at least one wounded man—I think there may be more— they can't very well go anywhere else. If Carlos does find Bryant Marlow's headquarters, I suggest that we gather a surprise posse and make a surprise attack on it and wipe it out—and a good part of the gang with it."

"You will never gather a posse," said Don Felipe, shaking his head. "There have been too many men killed. There is too much fear."

Blayde smiled a little.

"I couldn't announce one in advance, to be sure. But if Judge Harper and Matt Coulter privately approached men they know, telling them to go secretly to a certain

place, carrying arms, they might slip out of town one
by one. They might then join the men you can furnish,
Don Felipe. They might even be surprised and heart-
ened by their own number. If such a posse gathered in
secret, and if old Carlos does locate the gang's hideout,
such a posse might make a secret raid upon it. They
might even ride masked, though I do not like that. But
after a smashing blow at the Marlows, who could neither
anticipate nor meet it, they might gather courage to ride
openly back to Dallas and end the lawlessness that has
cost so many lives. It is the tactics of guerrillas or bandits, actually, used in the service of the law. But after
one victory there could be no revival of outlawry here,
because there would have been enough men around
who'd fought to end it."

"I do not like the tactics of bandits," said Don Felipe
distastefully.

"Bandits," said Blayde, "have made the law helpless.
I do not see why we should not use their own methods
to restore law."

Don Luis spoke firmly in approval. In half an hour he
rode over to Dallas to propose the plan to the only men
who had dared to express opposition to the Marlows and
who had so far escaped assassination.

Blayde waited restlessly to hear the reception Matt
Coulter and Judge Harper gave to his idea. It was asking
them to take a great risk, but they took great risk in
not kowtowing to Will Marlow anyhow.

He went out to the stable and made sure that Yank's
worn shoe had been replaced. He was greeted with grins
in the hacienda's blacksmith shop. And somehow the
atmosphere of approval around him wrenched at his feel-
ings. Small brown men who barely spoke English liked
him and admired him. There is nobody of Blayde's age
who does not hunger for approval. Here in the Hacienda
del Norte he was a hero. And it hurt because it meant
so much.

But it could not change the fact that he was on that
list of unforgiven and unforgivable rebels including Jef-

ferson Davis—still a close prisoner in Fortress Monroe—
and the members of his cabinet, many of whom had
escaped abroad, and such guerrillas as Quantrell and his
followers, and those sadists who had enjoyed themselves
as guards over prisoners of war.

Nothing could change the fact that he was technically
guilty of high treason against the United States for having carried out guerrilla action, in uniform, against one
of its officers after the ending of hostilities. And he could
be and would be eventually unmasked as an impostor
pretending to be a United States marshal. During that
imposture he had killed Cullen Marlow and two horse
thieves without legal authority. There could be no clearing up of all these items.

In the early afternoon he saw Antonia in her garden.
She looked at him with a sort of grave resolution.

"I was leaving," said Blayde harshly, "and they tell me
I can't leave without everything falling to pieces. Even
killing Will and Bryant Marlow won't finish the job
unless I get people worked up to where they'll combine
and fight for themselves."

Antonia nodded. Her eyes were curiously soft. "Yes,
Blayde."

"Your father and brother and Martin," said Blayde
as harshly as before, "are the people I count on most.
I need to work with them. But I can't do it if you—
bother me."

Antonia smiled very faintly. "You mean I mustn't try
to—overpower and kiss you?"

His hands clenched. She came barely above his shoulder, and she was slim and supple and utterly desirable.
She looked at him with a sort of forlorn twinkle in her
eyes. Suddenly he laughed reluctantly.

"Something like that. And if you tell Martin what
you've told me, I'll have to leave immediately. Understand?"

"Yes, Blayde." Then she did smile at him. "I won't
tell anybody that I've proposed to you and been refused.
But you can't stop me from scheming!"

He turned away. But he did not see very much as he
stirred uneasily about the hacienda's interior. Always
before his eyes there was the picture of Antonia, standing among the many-colored flowers of her garden. She
wore a white dress of some sort—the details were lost
upon him—and she would always remain in his memory
exactly like that.

The day passed. Luis rode back from Dallas. Blayde's
proposal of a secret posse, masked if necessary, had been
laid before Matt Coulter and Judge Harper in joint
executive session. Both were markedly unhappy at the
idea that honest men might feel it necessary to act in
secret for the protection of the peace of the community,
but they agreed reluctantly that perhaps it was the only
way the thing could be done. Of course, once as many
as a dozen men joined to strike a blow against the Marlow gang, there would be fifty more to join them. The
whole safety of any gang rule, even when it is called
a dictatorship or the benevolent guidance of a party,
lies in keeping the ruled people from daring to think
of revolt. That was why Walters had been murdered.
He had dared to think of honest men joining together
for their own safety, and he had dared to invite others
to join him.

The decision in Dallas was that it would be ticklish,
but it might be done. Matt Coulter and Judge Harper
would try it. But everything depended on their having
a specific thing to strike at, the instant men gathered.
Everything depended on the wizened old man who had
done the tracking the night before, and now was zestfully trying to repeat in his old age the high achievement
of his youth.

He was a very old man, this Carlos. No one knew his
last name. He had come to the hacienda years ago, and
had offered no information whatever about what he had
done or where he had lived before. But in time it was
noted that he spoke with absolute authority on two sub-
jects. One was the trailing of individual persons. The
other subject was the specific fate of each and every mem-

ber of a formerly notorious and now long extinct band
of Mexican brigands along the border.

It was rumored that his wife and daughter had been
carried off by that band, years before, when he was absent
from home. It was rumored that he had found their
bodies later. And it was said as a matter of legend that
for some time after the tragedy he had vanished often
from his regular haunts, and that his vanishings coin-
cided with remarkable accidents to the brigands in question. Members of the band were found shot dead. Some
died of drinking from poisoned wells. Once a group of
them was feasting very merrily in a house when it caught
on fire, and all the doors and windows were blocked,
and not one of them ever did get out. That particular
band of brigands had most remarkably dwindled, and
had finally ceased altogether to exist. But nobody said
outright that the old, quiet, dark-skinned man at the
Hacienda del Norte was responsible.

Now, with two other men to help him fight in case
of need, he was at work on the trail of the men who had
planned to ambush Blayde the night before. It was hoped
that he would uncover useful information.

In the late afternoon Blayde and Don Felipe and
Weatherby rode over to Dallas. They arrived near sunset, at just that moment of soft and quiet peacefulness
which is the perfection of dusk. Even the dust of the
streets seemed fragrant as their horses' hoofs stirred it,
and the smell of the cottonwood trees was pungent. There
was stirring and movement all through the town. Knots
of men formed and talked and dissolved, and other knots
formed and talked with no loss of disturbance. Some
seemed enraged, and some seemed amused. But the center
of all the excitement was the Chuckaway Saloon, whose
proprietor had been killed one day before. It appeared
to all the citizens of Dallas that it would be an appropriate gesture for them to patronize Bill Walters' widow's
inheritance—at least to provide her with a stake for her
immediate needs. Therefore the Chuckaway had such
patronage after its proprietor's death as it had never had

before, and it was in the beginning a delicate tribute to
a dead man and a furtive expression of sympathy for his
widow. But there had been developments.

When Blayde tethered Yank at the hitching rail and
went inside, he looked about the place and stiffened.
Then his face went flinty-hard and very pale. Quite automatically he moved to one side so that there was no one
behind him. His hands hung close by his sides. A smol-
dering light began to appear in his eyes. Because, at the
back of the saloon, he saw Matt Coulter and Judge
Harper at a table with Will Marlow, and apparently on
the best of terms. The gross, fat face of the eldest of the
Marlow brothers was relaxed and complacent. Blayde
said quietly:

"Don Felipe, will you and my brother ride back to the
hacienda and tell Don Luis of this development? It appears—"

At that instant Judge Harper looked up and saw
Blayde. He said a quick word to Coulter and rose. He
came toward Blayde, elbowing a way through the crowd.
Blayde watched him coldly. Then he noticed Coulter's
expression. It was amused. It was relieved. It was not
menacing. It was not guilty. Which was startling.

Judge Harper grimaced as he drew near to Blayde.

"Dammit," he said peevishly, "I think we need you
badly, Marshal. Get that look off your face! We're not
crooking you, but Matt Coulter and I have told more
lies this afternoon than I ever heard a man tell on a
witness stand."

Don Felipe said frostily, "I think, Judge Harper, that
to see you associating with Will Marlow is enough to
excuse any expression—"

The Judge sputtered at him. He waved his arms. He
seethed, but he spoke in a low tone.

"I'm doing it for law and order, dammit!" he said
furiously. "Dallas has been lawless, like a damned wild-
West town, and I won't have it! And I don't like the
idea of any posse riding behind masks, either! Matt Coulter and I, we're working to organize a posse right out in

the open. D'you see Will Marlow back there? We're
working on him to head it! Against his brother Bryant!"

"You joke!" said Don Felipe coldly.

"I've been lying all afternoon," said the Judge angrily,
"and that's no joke. Dammit, don't you see, Marshal, that
this is a better idea than you proposed?"

Blayde tore his eyes from Will Marlow. He shook his
head.

"Listen," sputtered the Judge, "we've been telling Will
Marlow he should be mayor of Dallas! We've been telling him he's the one leading citizen who can lead the
town's citizens! We've been telling him every man in
Dallas is thirsting to have Will Marlow lead him to put
down lawlessness!"

The flinty look left Blayde's face. His lips twitched a
little.

"I see," he said dryly. "I wouldn't have thought of
that."

"It's your idea, made practical—and with no masks,"
said the Judge. Then he added, "But the lies! The only
reason I'm not a perjurer is that what I said to Will Marlow I didn't say in a courtroom. We've been listening
to him, pouring drinks into him, while he told us what
a grief Bryant has been to him, and what a noble character he is—him, Will Marlow! And how he's grieved
and prayed that Bryant would quit helling around. *And*
he's been talking about Cullen and saying how he can't
blame you for killing him, because if you hadn't, Cullen
would have been a murderer—as if he wasn't!"

Don Felipe said with dignity, "I do not understand
this."

"I do," said Blayde dryly. "Men have been afraid to
speak or even think against Bryant Marlow's followers,
for fear of Will Marlow. A posse might have been impossible, even a masked one. But nobody will be afraid
to join a posse that Will Marlow heads!"

"But what will such a posse do?" demanded Don
Felipe with scorn. "Under his leadership—"

"The second thing it would do," said Blayde genially,

"is hang Will Marlow. Get fifty men together with arms in their hands and knowledge that every one of them is ready to fight Bryant, and what will they do to Will?"

Don Felipe's face was a study as the idea took hold. "But—will he accept the idea of leading a posse?"

"Accept, the devil!" snapped Judge Harper. "What we're trying to do right now is convince him that *we'll* accept it! *I* know what's in his mind. He'd like to go through with it, lead us on a grand and useless foray after Bryant—whom he'd tip off in advance—get elected mayor of Dallas, and then settle down in a legally air-tight position with Bryant back on the job outside of town running lawlessness and him on the inside running the law! He'd own Dallas County with a lawyer-proof title within six months. Don't you think he believes he's smart enough to work things out just like that? And won't he jump at it?"

Blayde said, "If he's vain enough, perhaps."

"I won't testify against myself," said Judge Harper darkly, "but the plain and fancy prevarication I've done to build up his vanity is masterly stuff, Marshal. We've got him teetering. You come over to the table in a minute or two and finish him up. Prod him a little. Understand? And we'll swing it!"

He went bustling back to the table at which Matt Coulter sat with Will Marlow. Don Felipe said remotely: "I am not sure that I approve."

Then a worried-looking man said in a low tone to Blayde, "Marshal, what do you think of this idea Judge Harper an' Matt Coulter are spreadin'? To make Will Marlow mayor of Dallas?"

"You could do worse," said Blayde. "You might choose Bryant."

The worried-looking man said hopefully, "They say he'd chase Bryant out. Take a posse and go get him."

"He might offer to," said Blayde detachedly. "Anyhow, if you did form a posse—a good, strong, well-armed posse—do you think he could keep you from getting Bryant if you wanted to?"

The worried-looking man blinked. Then he said in sudden harshness, "That's right! Yeah! That's right, Marshal!"

"I think I'll ask him if he means to try," said Blayde.

He shouldered his way through the crowded saloon to where Will Marlow sat. The grossly fat man was partly but not wholly drunk. He had taken enough, surely, to put most men under the table. Undoubtedly he felt it. But he was more nearly drunk with flattery than with whisky. A man does not go outside the law for no reason at all. Especially he does not undertake the labor and danger and sweating anxiety of heading an outlaw band for a reward of loot alone. He does it for the gratification of a vanity that insists that he is remarkable, much too smart to be stodgy and merely earn his money, so brilliant that he forces or induces others to pay tribute to his vastly greater wisdom and skill and courage and remarkable qualities generally. And, of course, to be admired and flattered and feared and dreaded is his actual reward.

A killer, a braggart, a fool of criminal stripe kills other men that heads may turn to look at him, or so that he can think with satisfaction that his name is on many lips. Will Marlow had become the brains of bushwhackers to have the fine high satisfaction of eminence among his own kind. But now he had been exposed to hours of reasonably skilled adulation from men who had never before yielded him even respect. At the beginning he was suspicious. But it was too perfectly what his whole nature craved for him to resist it overlong.

As Blayde drew near, Matt Coulter was saying:

"A job like that takes a man of big caliber. It's time a strong stand was taken here in Dallas, and you're the man to take it!"

Will Marlow swayed a little where he sat. His face was just a little slack.

"You don't have to call me Mr. Marlow," he said generously. "Jus' call me Will."

"Yes, sir!" said Matt Coulter. "As mayor of Dallas,

His Honor Mayor Marlow of Dallas, you'd enforce respect for the law!"

Marlow said almost tearfully, "But there's my brother Bryant! Nobody'd believe I'd act against Bryant. There'sh people right now—"

Blayde loomed above the table. He looked down grimly at one of the two remaining men he was resolved to kill. Will Marlow looked up with slightly bleary eyes. Matt Coulter said:

"Evening, Marshal." He paused, and added as if defiantly, "A bunch of us citizens have been feeling out Mr. Marlow about running for mayor of Dallas."

Judge Harper said acidly, "It's about time we had a go-getter in office. A city like ours needs a modern, Eastern-style administration with no wild West about it. Dallas is going to be a great city! She'll have rock-oil lamps in her streets, and pavements, and it wouldn't surprise me if we didn't get around to indoor water closets! We'll get the electric telegraph, and after that there'll come a railroad. Yes, sir! With a go-getter mayor, it wouldn't surprise me any to get appropriation from the Legislature to hoist up the snags in the Trinity River and someday have a line of steamboats running right to Dallas. But it takes a man to lead in that kind of civic enterprise. If Mr. Marlow will run for mayor—"

The part Blayde should play was self-evident, and he saw that Marlow was ripe. But he almost despised himself for falling in with such trickery, despite its sardonic humor, rather than simply and forthrightly challenging Marlow to get out his pistol and fight for his life. Nevertheless, he said:

"No use, Judge. He won't be available to serve."

"And why not?"

"I'll have him in jail," said Blayde.

Will Marlow looked up pathetically. "That's a mighty poor joke, Marshal."

Judge Harper, grimacing, said the appropriate next line, "You shouldn't make irresponsible statements, Marshal!"

"He's working with Bryant Marlow right now," said Blayde coldly. "He's the brains of the Marlow gang. His brother tried to bushwhack me last night—lured me out to be shot down. And he was in on it!"

Will Marlow cried indignantly, "That's a—"

Blayde tensed. Will Marlow stopped short. Again Blayde despised himself, that he should feel it insupportable that a murderer should call him a liar. But he said furiously:

"Just what is it?"

Will Marlow hesitated. Then he protested shrilly, "Somebody's been lyin' to you, Marshal! Anybody says I was ever joined up with Bryant in any criminal doin's, I'll sue him for libel!"

"Your offices were used yesterday for two attempts at murder," snapped Blayde. "One of them almost included you! That wound on your cheek that you've got covered with plaster—did you get that by having nothing to do with your brothers?"

There was dead silence in the Chuckaway. Every man listened. Will Marlow sweated suddenly. He was in a cleft stick. Blayde stood over him, deadly and raging inside. To defy him was impossible. But—

"It's Bryant's doing," said Will Marlow in a voice several tones higher than normal. "He's a renegade. He's followed me everywhere, making a mock of my law-abiding principles. He's made me suspected. He's tried to ruin me. He—he— If you want to know, Marshal, it wouldn't surprise me any if he hadn't sent Cullen to kill me yesterday! He come out of that door shooting at me. A bullet hit me before you cut him down."

There was not a man in the place who wholly believed that. But only Blayde dared show his scorn. Then Matt Coulter said stoutly:

"He's got you there, Marshal! There was Cullen aiming to wipe out his own brother on Bryant's orders! How'd he get hit if Cullen wasn't aiming at him? You're wrong, Marshal. Will Marlow's going to be the next mayor of Dallas! He don't hold with outlaws. Why, he was talking today about putting up a reward for Bryant's arrest!"

Judge Harper interposed deftly, "You can't say Will Marlow is in cahoots with outlaws if he puts up a reward for them. And that will stand in court!"

"He hasn't done it yet," said Blayde. "Shall I hold my breath until he does?"

There was a tense, waiting silence. Marlow said uneasily:

"It ain't easy, brother putting the dead mark on brother. . . ."

Matt Coulter whooped. "You hear that, gentlemen? Will Marlow, the next mayor of Dallas, puts up a reward for his brother Bryant, and he makes it dead or alive! That's a big man, gentlemen! He's big enough for mayor of Dallas! He's big enough for governor! He's big enough—"

There was a murmur, and then almost an uproar. The eyes of Will Marlow went uneasily here and there. But men were shouting. He was approved. He was admired. He got to his feet.

"That's right," he said shakily. "I'm offering two thousand dollars for my brother Bryant—"

Coulter bellowed, "Dead or alive!"

Blayde felt a little bit sick inside. The whole crowded saloon was in an uproar now. Men rushed outside to spread the news. There was a man at the head of the bar shouting, "I'm joining Marshal Weatherby's posse to hunt down Bryant Marlow! Who's joining up?" Other voices bellowed. The shouting man produced a sheet of paper. He signed it. Other men signed. It was astonishing how many men thrust forward to sign their names to an exact duplicate of the document that had got Bill Walters murdered in this same saloon only thirty hours before. There was shouting down the street, where a missionary reported Will Marlow's action. He was the center, here, of a group of ardent fools who pressed drinks upon him and wrung his hand.

And Blayde forced his way out of the saloon and stood

in the night beyond it. For some reason he shivered. Perhaps it was scorn. Perhaps it was contempt. Perhaps it was shame that he was associated, even in enmity, with a man like that.

There were five of them gathered in the darkness to one side of the saloon, while shoutings filled the air.

"Dirty business," said Blayde, clamping his teeth. "They were afraid to speak out before. Now all of a sudden every man in town has signed his own death warrant. He knows it's his death warrant if Will Marlow changes his mind. And so they'll fight. Together!"

Judge Harper said acidly: "Wasn't that the idea? We humans are fools, and it takes tricksters to make us act like we ought to. But I hate to think of the lies I've told this day!"

A little brown man came riding into town, scanning the horses at the hitching racks in the darkness. He recognized Yank, and then the horses of Don Felipe and Weatherby. He dismounted.

"Carlos," said Don Felipe quietly.

The brown man came to him, grinning. He spoke softly, in Spanish. Don Felipe said quietly to Blayde:

"My servant, the tracker, found the place where the Marlow gang lies hidden. One of my men has gone back to the hacienda to get those of my *vaqueros* who will join the fight. I think it is time to say that the place is known. While the citizens are ready for battle—before they can think—"

"I'll attend to that," said Judge Harper zestfully. "Dammit, it's going to feel funny to tell the truth for a change. I'll tip Matt Coulter off first of all."

He rushed away. Don Felipe said very slowly:

"Don Martin, I am accustomed to giving orders to my servants. While I am with them, they will naturally take orders from no one else. If I am not with them, they will take orders from you. I have done much fighting in my life. This I give over to you. I shall go back to the hacienda and tell Antonia to pray for you, because I am sure that you will be in the forefront of the fighting."

Then he nodded and said quietly, "Perhaps I shall join her. I should grieve very much if anything happened to you. Not only on Antonia's account, but because I should not like to lose you as my son-in-law. I beg you to be as careful as is consistent with courage."

He mounted and rode briskly away down the street. A buzzing, humming noise began in the Chuckaway. It turned to that completely indescribable sound of men suddenly discovering that they are many, and all of them resolute and enraged. Judge Harper had passed on the news that the hiding place of the Marlow gang was discovered.

Men began to run toward their horses. The posse was forming in furious haste. It was the most deadly sort of posse that could possibly be imagined.

It did not need anybody to organize it. It organized itself.

Chapter Eleven

THERE WAS tumult and confusion everywhere. The whole atmosphere of the town was changed. Men who had been fearful because their neighbors seemed cowed suddenly discovered that their neighbors had been fearful because they themselves seemed cowed. Despair had been a carefully nurtured plague. Now men saw courage in each other's eyes, and exultation filled them. It required expression, and the way to express it was at hand. They began to appear with rifles. They began to ride toward the center of town on the horses they kept in private stables behind their homes. There was clamor at the livery stable. Patrons fought to be first to get their saddles from the racks, and to put them on the horses presumably turned into the corral for the night. Ropes snaked through the darkness. Horses fought the ropes, and men swore. But mounted figures began to ride away from the scene of that confusion.

A knot of eager inquirers surrounded the little dark man who had brought word to Don Felipe of the Marlow gang's hideout. They had set drinks before him, and they were flinging hungry questions at him, in English and in haphazard Spanish.

Matt Coulter came out of the Chuckaway, shaking with laughter. He had a lean man with him. He found Blayde in the darkness, and shook his hand violently.

"I knew it! I knew I'd seen you somewheres! I tol' Don Luis I knew it! But heah's the man who'll back me up. Colonel, suh, heah's one of your men from the Fifth Georgia! He set back an' watched you tame Will Marlow by just lookin' at him, an' by Gawd, suh, when you went outside he came over to me, and he said, 'That's my old colonel, by Gawd, an' if theah's fightin' he'll find it, an' he'll win it, too!' "

The lean man grinned at Blayde.

"Colonel Hollister, suh!" he said exuberantly. "Matt Coulter told me he was mighty sure it was you, suh, but I couldn't believe you'd be down thisaway. You know me?"

"Yes," said Blayde quietly. "Sergeant Gayle. Fourth troop. You wouldn't keep your carbine clean except the barrel and the lock, and you could find a chicken on top of a flagpole—and steal it, too!"

The lean man howled with gratified laughter. He slapped his thighs.

"Yes, suh! That's me! And I'm ridin' with you tonight. The old Fifth Georgia's ridin'!"

Blayde said, "You'll take my orders?" But there was no need to ask that. "Get this posse moving. Pick up the guide—that little Mexican who brought the news. Get going. Here's a good man. Martin Weatherby. Work with him. Martin, get mounted and help get this thing in motion. They're too enthusiastic now. They're making too much noise. Get them on the road. Sergeant Gayle, sort them out as you go. I'll follow in a moment."

"Yes, suh, Colonel! I'll pass the word around that we got the fightin'est colonel in the whole Confederate Army with us! Lordy, Colonel! You shoulda seen Will Marlow's face when I told him you was my old colonel, Reb Hollister!"

Blayde said harshly, "He heard that? Where is he?"

"Clumb on a hawss, suh. Somewheres around."

Blayde swore. Once. Then he said savagely, "Get this mob moving! Coulter! Martin! Gayle! Get them moving!" To Martin he added in what was almost an agony of frustration, "Once he knows I'm Hollister, it may take months to find him again!"

He was trembling. But there were suddenly men who had orders to give. They moved about, shouting their commands. The commands were identical. A knot of twenty men swept down the street with the small Mexican in their midst. They cried out triumphantly. Other mounted men fell in behind them. From far down the street horses scampered to join the troop. Men not yet

mounted tightened their girths, swearing furiously in
their haste, and vaulted into the saddles and went tearing
after the forward groups. More men ran out of saloons
where they had taken a last drink, mounted, and went
spurring furiously after the rest.

There was a diminishing mutter of horses' hoofs moving off into the distance. The main street of Dallas was
empty and still. There were still some lights in the saloons,
but the hitching racks were empty, save for Yank, and
there was not one moving figure anywhere in sight.

Blayde stood trembling in the darkness. Then he took
a deep breath and walked quietly toward the sign that
said:

WM. MARLOW AND COMPANY
Land Bought and Sold
Mortgages — Insurance

He reached the bottom of the stair. He moved to put
his foot upon it. Then he hesitated and went around to
the back of the building. Moonlight shone down there.
He saw that the window through which a man had
jumped the day before was no longer an open space. The
heavy wooden shutters that normally hung open were now
closed. Tightly. Nobody could open them without at least
some slight noise.

It was very quiet indeed. Yank looked very lonely, tied
to the hitching rail on the other side of the moonlit
street. It was incredible that a town could be so still. It
seemed as if all the world held its breath to listen.

Blayde stood in the angular shadows at the very base of
the building that held Will Marlow's office. Outside, from
across the street, he had seen a momentary glow in the
dark interior. Somebody in the office had struck a match
to light something to smoke. An intruder would not do
that. Only a man who waited for the owner of the office
to return would do so—and most waiting men would
have made a light to see by. But there would be one man
who would wait in Will Marlow's office without calling

attention to himself. That man would be Will Marlow's
brother.

It was inconceivable that it could be anybody else. Not
Will Marlow. He'd been seen on a horse. He wouldn't
know that anyone waited for him. Judge Harper and
Coulter had been with him all day. He'd have taken off,
ahead of the posse. To hunt him down was a new purpose
that might take almost forever, but it would be done.

Meanwhile, there had been a match struck in Will Marlow's office.

Stillness. Darkness. Moonlight. Blayde felt the weapons
in his holsters. His eyes glowing, he moved.

Then there was a sound. Someone was coming out.
Coming down. To a man uninformed, the tumult of the
gathering posse would have been alarming and inexplica-
ble. He would stay close until it had gone. Then he'd come
down and get his horse from wherever it was and get out
of town.

The platform at the top of the stairs squeaked. Then
someone came almost noiselessly down the steps. Blayde
trembled violently. Veins throbbed and pulsed in his tem-
ples. He suddenly drew a deep breath and forced himself
to be calm.

Step by step the man descended. He reached the bottom. Blayde saw him silhouetted against the moonlit dust
of the middle of the street. Lanky. Lean. Graceful. The
clean-cut outline of his figure showed holsters at his hips,
a ragged short beard on his chin.

Blayde moved toward him.

The man looked up and down the street. He was
puzzled.

Blayde came from behind him. He said with soft ferocity, "Bryant?"

The man whirled. Blayde continued to move toward
him.

"Who's that?" snapped the man.

"The name's Hollister," said Blayde. "Blayde Hollister."

A flame leaped toward him. Something slapped his

side. There was a forming cloud of smoke, expanding swiftly. Blayde fired, and fired again. The sound of shots echoed back and forth in the deserted, moonlit street. The two small figures of men seemed to stand in white clouds among which lightning flashes flickered redly. Beneath the great hemisphere that was the sky they were very small indeed, and their lightnings were miniature. But to their own ears the thunders were deafening and the lightnings were death.

The lean man's arm dropped and he staggered. The re-echoings of the shots continued to race back and forth between the buildings as he collapsed limply to the ground. He lay still. But he breathed, with difficulty.

Blayde advanced upon him. The gaunt, bearded face looked up. A rusty voice said:

"Got me." It was vaguely wondering. "What for?"

"What for?" raged Blayde. "My name's Hollister! You murdered my parents and my sister! You killed her yourself!"

The voice was faint, but detachedly amused. "Don't remember, fella. You put up—signs. Reward. Why?"

Blayde felt a horrible frustration. It was intolerable that this man should die without knowing for what reason he had been killed. He panted at him, chokingly flinging details at him, absurdly reminding him.

The dying man said more faintly, "Oh. . . . That one. Will wanted her. I carted her off for him. . . . She got a gun an' was shootin'. Will hollered not to kill her, just cripple her. . . . But she had spunk. I kind of ad-mired her. . . . So I shot her dead. Will was awful mad. . . ."

The voice grew very faint indeed, while Blayde stood above the man he had trailed so far. There was the same detached amusement as the voice went on, growing ever weaker.

"Will ain't nice to women. Takin' the gang tonight to get that Robles gal. . . . Figures Robles is likely to be dangerous, trainin' them Mexes to fight like Confeds, an' gettin' in marshals. . . . Wipe him out an' folks'll be scared."

The eyes of the man in the dust of the street ceased to be bright and mocking. They were still. They looked sightlessly up at the stars.

Suddenly, everything was clear. Not only the true leadership and the true crime for which he had still to impose a just penalty, but the actual result of the grisly comedy played here tonight. Matt Coulter and the Judge had schemed zestfully to turn Will Marlow's criminal eminence and terrorism back upon him, to make him raise the very posse that would destroy him. But while they flattered and cajoled and deceived him, his own counterstroke was already planned and waiting. He would, to be sure, have led the posse tonight, to attack the utterly empty hideout of his own and his brother's followers. But while the posse rode valiantly upon a useless errand, Bryant Marlow would have raided the Hacienda del Norte—and most of its men were absent with the posse. He would have left the hacienda a burned-out shell. He would have done such mass murder, committed such a massacre, as should terrify all men past ever daring to oppose the Marlows in Dallas County again. And Will Marlow would have the most perfect of alibis.

He had intended, undoubtedly, to slip into his office for a moment before the posse left, to give last-minute instructions to Bryant, waiting there. But the knowledge that Reb Hollister was in Dallas, and that Reb Hollister was the man who had killed his brother Cullen and proved his deadliness amply both before and since that fact, and that Reb Hollister was somehow privy to the forming of the posse and had some purpose of his own behind it, and that his one purpose in life was to kill the three Marlows—that was too much. Will Marlow had fled.

But even that was cunning itself. He believed his enemy riding with the posse. He believed Bryant either with the outlaw gang or quite safely hidden in his own darkened office, which he would surely leave in safety once the posse had ridden out of town. Perhaps he did not even think of Bryant. But he would think of Antonia. Marshal Weatherby was to marry her. Marshal Weatherby was his

enemy, Blayde Hollister, and the killer of his brother
Cullen. With everything ready for the raid on the hacienda and with its defenders away.

Will Marlow might flee. But on his way he would do
what mad-dog damage he could.

Blayde stood motionless for seconds. Then, suddenly,
he was running. He raged into the Chuckaway Saloon. It
was empty, with all its lights burning. He ran to another
saloon, and another. The business section of Dallas was
emptied of human life. Then he remembered the corral.
There was a fourteen-year-old Negro boy still there, bath-
ing the injured hoof of a horse. He dripped water over
it into a bucket, and sopped it up to drip again.

Blayde shook him into scared alertness. He panted the
warning Bryant Marlow had given him. He thrust greenbacks into the colored boy's hands. He made him repeat
the warning. He made him swear to ride, to overtake the
posse, to bring it to the hacienda.

"Tell them," he panted. "Sergeant Gayle. Daniel
Weatherby. Coulter. Tell them! Give them this to prove
I sent you!"

He ripped off the badge of a United States marshal and
thrust it into the boy's hand. He watched the boy go racing off into the night, his horse's hoofs pounding in panic-
stricken tempo.

Then Blayde ran to Yank and rode for the Hacienda
del Norte. It seemed the longest journey he had ever
taken in his life.

When he came in sight of it, lights burned wholly as
usual. He used his spurs, desperately praying that he was
in time. With the gate closed and the men within it
alerted, even with only Don Luis and Don Felipe and
himself, there could be a defense against any gang of outlaws that could be gathered. A man who fights for loot
is not notably courageous. It takes a cause, a faith, a belief
of some sort to make a man face flying lead. Outlaws and
bushwhackers achieve their feats by surprise and stealth
and ruthlessness, never by ferocity or nerve.

He was half a mile away when he saw a clump of

tethered horses. They must be the mounts of the outlaws, who had crept up to the gate on foot. There would surely be some man among them to boast of his ability to creep up and knife a sentry without his victim's having the least forewarning. There would be others to creep within the gate, once a sentry was disposed of. The fact that there was so far no alarm was proof—

There was a scream and a shot. Then a ripple of crackling explosions, muted by the distance. Flames leaped up somewhere.

Blayde made inarticulate noises in his throat and spurred mercilessly, though Yank had never failed to give willingly to the last of his strength. He went pounding down the last incline to the hacienda, and a figure started up in his path, crying out, and Blayde leaned from the saddle to strike with the barrel of his pistol. That man, at least, died with his skull crushed in.

Then Blayde was inside the courtyard. And there was pandemonium there. From the quarters of the *vaqueros* there came shrieks. A shotgun boomed. From within the house proper there came the sound of a revolver blasting itself empty. A heavy shutter somewhere fell with a crash. Don Felipe's voice, shouting angrily and commandingly. He heard Antonia.

He fired at a man with a torch and saw him fall. He plunged into the dwelling through one of the tall windows to the great hall. Someone cried out and he panted:
"Antonia!"

She dashed out a candle, and a pistol spurted flame from the doorway and a voice cursed filthily. Then there were crashes behind him, and the room was utterly dark. Antonia had dropped the heavy wooden shutters that had been installed in ancient days to make every part of the hacienda a separate fortress to be defended to the death.

"Blayde?" she called in terror. "Is it you?"

Again a pistol flashed, and its sound echoed between the paneled hardwood walls.

"I'm here," panted Blayde, shooting at the flash.

He flung himself away from his own fire, and two

weapons blazed at it. He snapped another shot at them.
He heard the unpleasant sound of a bullet striking flesh,
even in the ringing echoes of the explosion.

Overhead a firearm crashed, and he heard Don Felipe's
voice. Someone began to race down the stairs. Blayde
shouted:

"Luis! Go back! I'm here!"

Explosions struck through his voice. Bullets smashed
near him. There was a snarling sound, and somehow he
knew that it was Will Marlow somewhere in this room.
A terrible fury filled him so that for an instant he was
not able to do anything but gasp in that awful, killing
rage. It seemed that his skull would split with the pres-
sure of the hatred in it. He knew that something had
touched his shoulder, and he felt warm blood trickling
down, but it did not hurt.

Overhead there was more shooting. Outside, a man
screamed. There were yells, and bangings, and all the
disconnected and irrelevant and improbable noises of
deadly fighting done in snatches, as when prowling men
came upon a woman armed with a knife or her husband's
shotgun, or when an old man—this happened—posted
himself in a stable doorway and zestfully, with veined and
shaky hands, made use of a shotgun and half a box of
shells at any target that showed. There was a boy, too,
who had a very light rifle suited to his years, and with a
pounding heart made use of it to earn the commendations
of his elders when they should return.

But in the great hall of the hacienda there was a deadly hunt in progress. Blayde heard a muttering, which must
have been close to the door. Then an infinitely soft rustling close to him. He heard soft, panting breaths.

Antonia clung to him, patting him with trembling
hands. He put his lips to her ear.

"Get behind something big," he whispered. Then he
whispered again. "The piano? Cushions? To throw at the
keys?"

He felt her nod. Her fingers twisted themselves into his.
She tugged gently. They crawled.

There was light. Someone outside in the hallway
scratched a match. There was instantly a shot from above
and a man made agonized gasping sounds. A fusillade
poured up the steps toward the second floor. Luis, halted
on the stair by Blayde's warning shout, had waited to be
of use.

A woman began to scream shrilly outside. A shotgun
boomed.

Blayde felt Antonia reaching up. She thrust a cushion,
pulled from a chair seat, into his hands. He breathed into
her ear:

"You throw. Make the keys sound, as if someone
brushed against them."

There was a queer feeling of tension in the slim body
beside him. The piano tinkled faintly, as if someone
bumped against its keys and hastily moved away.

Three weapons spouted flame at the noise. Blayde got
in two shots—aimed ones—where the flashes came from.
He dragged Antonia swiftly away.

The screams outside stopped abruptly. A man shouted
triumphantly, and his shout was cut off in the middle as
if a knife had gone into him. More shots from overhead.

Then, suddenly, there was stillness. Everywhere, over
all the hacienda, there was no sound at all. In the great
hall the silence was ear-cracking. Once, once only, there
was a stirring somewhere. Then a growling, snarling,
half-mad voice. It spoke from behind something, so that
it seemed to come from everywhere at once. It was Will
Marlow's voice. It cursed thickly and revoltingly. It threat-
ened. With a ghastly assurance of success, it promised
unspeakable things. . . .

Antonia pressed against Blayde, shivering. He put his
arm about her. In the utter darkness, with a man gone
mad with fury and disappointment even now planning
some trick to kill them both, Blayde kissed her.

It was altogether an incredible sensation to feel soft '
lips pressing desperately against his while he waited for
the explosion of a revolver in the dark.

The explosions came, a furious, crashing, deafening

drumfire of shots, in which Will Marlow raked the room from side to side with the bullets of both his pistols. Blayde flung himself before Antonia. He heard a hammer click.

He threw himself at the sound. He almost missed. Then he caught hold, and a gross, sweating body with a coating of fat over monstrous muscles was locked in a death grip with him.

Then the great hall resounded to writhing, gasping sounds, to the curiously inadequate noise of shoe soles scuffling on the floor. Once there was the peculiar noise of spur rowels biting into hardwood. There was the impact of something upon flesh. A growling sound rose and rose in triumph to a bestial bellow of victory.

Then there came a peculiar smacking noise. Then there was no more struggling.

Outside, shouts. Cries of terror. Sudden rushings, and sudden spiteful further shots, and the shrill outcries of women and vengeful shooting from overhead.

And then the distant thunder of hoofs. They were coming nearer. The sounds of battle dwindled and cries of hatred took their place. And then there was a rippling of shots outside the gateway, and the sound of mounted men riding in, and yet another flurry of shooting—very brief—and then voices bellowed:

"Don Felipe! Marshal!"

There was still no sound in the great hall, but someone came down the stairs. He entered the hall and struck a match. It was Don Luis, Antonia's brother, his shirt front stained and blood dripping from his fingers.

He looked inscrutably at his sister. She was weeping. There were two dead men in the room. There was Will Marlow in a contorted heap five feet from where she wept. But she sobbed on in a passion of relief and joy and gratitude, and Blayde Hollister held her in his arms, the two of them sitting most awkwardly upon the floor. And Antonia pressed desperately close to him, and wept, and kissed him, and he kissed her also in absolute obliviousness of the interruption.

Don Luis' hand shook a little as he lighted a candle. He looked at Will Marlow. He said detachedly:

"It does not seem that he is quite dead. It is deplorable."

He reached down and took the weapons that were within the reach of the last of the Marlow brothers. Then Blayde stirred. He got unsteadily to his feet.

"If you wish," said Don Luis detachedly, "I will go out. I am not sure that he is still alive. It merely seems so. I might be mistaken. The question can be settled—later."

Blayde said thickly, "No. That's the posse outside. Turn him over to them. I—I'm done with killing."

Don Luis looked at his sister. He helped her to her feet.

"Fortunately," he said with stately dignity, "you are engaged to be married to him. It is still most improper. But I shall say nothing, because you are to marry him."

He walked out of the room. Don Felipe came down the stairs from above. He looked in, and some of the drawn look on his face vanished as he saw Antonia clearly unharmed. He went on. He stepped over a man on the floor in the hallway—Don Luis' handiwork from the stairs. He went on to greet the members of the posse.

Antonia looked at Blayde with shining eyes.

"I am disgraced," she said shakily, "unless you marry me now, Blayde. My brother— We are a very conservative family. You have—kissed me and—he will insist—" But she was radiant. There was blood upon her dress—Blayde's. There was even a stain upon her bare arm. But she looked at Blayde and smiled happily and said, "Truly, Blayde, I did not scheme this!"

Weatherby was very pale indeed at breakfast. The servant came in, very formal in his manner but with a bright light of triumph in his eyes. He placed letters before Don Felipe. Don Felipe examined them and handed an envelope to Blayde. It was a thick envelope. Blayde glanced at it and handed it to Weatherby.

"It is from the attorney general of the United States," said Don Felipe, "and you do not open it?"

Blayde shook his head. Weatherby opened the envelope. He looked at the document inside.

"Blayde," he said suddenly, swallowing. Don Felipe stared at the unfamiliar name. "Blayde," said Weatherby again, "after Callao, I returned that five thousand dollars to the attorney general. I wrote what you had done at Callao. I wrote to my father and told—about you and everything. He went to Washington. He went to the President. The attorney general went with him. They told him the whole story, just the way it happened. The President has sent you this."

He laid the sheet on the table before Blayde. It was a large oblong of impressive foolscap paper. The heading was: "The Government of the United States." Underneath, in a neat curving line of rather elaborate type, there was a second heading: "Certificate of Pardon." There was a paragraph of fine italic type, with blank spaces filled in with a pen. There was a second, shorter paragraph of italics. Underneath was the signature of the President of the United States.

"That is not pay," said Weatherby, in a strained voice, "for anything you ever did for me, Blayde. It's an apology from the President for what a Federal captain did in Valdosta, Georgia, and it's a letter of thanks for what you did in Callao, and—and you can't be angry with me for it, because all I did was tell the truth about what you are and what you did!"

Blayde went pale. But his eyes looked miserable, anyhow.

"If I didn't feel like a scoundrel before," he said, "this would make me!"

Antonia smiled at him. She reached out and put her hand on Weatherby's arm.

"Martin!" she said remorsefully. "I am so sorry!"

Weatherby tried to grin, but he did it with his lips only.

"I shall always be proud," said Antonia honestly, "that you wished to marry me, Martin. I do not think that any woman has ever had so much reason to be proud. To have you care for me, and Blayde also . . . it is something to make anyone grateful."

Don Felipe stared from one to the other.

"But—what is this?" he demanded indignantly. "I see that the paper is a pardon. It is an impertinence! If my son-in-law-to-be has ever been accused of anything for which a government would feel obliged to pardon him, I will take the matter up! It is an insult! I shall protest it as an affront! *Hijo mio*," he said hotly to Blayde, "I will not endure it that a government—a president—anyone at all—"

Don Luis grinned quietly.

"*Padre mio*," he said gently, "let us go into another room. Don Daniel has something to say to you." Then he turned to Weatherby and offered his hand. "Don Martin, I did not think I could ever like a Yankee. You are not to be my brother-in-law. But will you be my friend?"

Weatherby stammered. Don Luis rose. His father, staring bewilderedly, accepted the hint. Weatherby stood up.

Then Antonia stood up also. She went to Weatherby and put her hands on his shoulders.

"Martin," she said softly, "I love you very dearly. Not only because you brought me Blayde, but for yourself. You are my dearest brother from now on and for always."

She kissed him. And she meant it. Weatherby flushed to the roots of his hair, and his ears were almost incandescent. Then he went very pale, and stumbled from the room. Blayde said awkwardly:

"Don Felipe, you should talk to him about railroads. He knows more of such things than I do."

Then the door closed. Antonia sat down beside Blayde. She looked at him very happily.

"Now everything is settled. Everything, Blayde! And now I can take care of you. You were hurt again last night. You have so many wounds! You must hurry and get well!" Then she flushed and said, "It is nice that they left us alone. We can have breakfast together. It—it—"

Blayde suddenly stared at her, in surprise at a remarkable thought that had occurred to him.

"Antonia!" he said amazedly. "Do you realize that this is only the first time? That we'll be having breakfast together all the rest of our lives?"

Antonia said softly, "I know. It's nice. Now eat your breakfast."